"You're a good man, Kip, and you're an even better brother."

She smiled. "I don't know many men who would let their brother and two little boys move in with him when he already had a mother and a sister to take care of."

Kip glanced over at Nicole, her soft smile easing into his soul. Then puzzlement took over. "Why are you telling me this? Aren't you supposed to be making me out to be the bad guy?" His eyes skimmed over her face, then met her gaze.

She didn't look away. "You're not the bad guy."

Kip didn't reply, not sure what to make of her. Was she flirting with him?

"You just happen to be caught in a bad situation." Then she looked away.

What was she doing? Was she playing him?

He wasn't sure what to think. Then he glanced over at her. She was watching him again. That had been happening a lot lately, but this time as their eyes met, he felt a deeper, surprising emotion.

More than appeal. More than attraction....

Books by Carolyne Aarsen

Love Inspired

A Bride at Last
The Cowboy's Bride
*A Family-Style Christmas
*A Mother at Heart
*A Family at Last
A Hero for Kelsey
Twin Blessings
Toward Home
Love Is Patient
A Heart's Refuge
Brought Together by Baby
A Silence in the Heart
Any Man of Mine
Yuletide Homecoming
Finally a Family
A Family for Luke
The Matchmaking Pact
Close to Home
Cattleman's Courtship
Cowboy Daddy

*Stealing Home

CAROLYNE AARSEN

and her husband, Richard, live on a small ranch in northern Alberta, where they have raised four children and numerous foster children and are still raising cattle. Carolyne crafts her stories in her office with a large west-facing window through which she can watch the changing seasons while struggling to make her words obey.

Lori
miller

Cowboy Daddy
Carolyne Aarsen

Steeple
Hill®

Published by Steeple Hill Books™

STEEPLE HILL BOOKS

Steeple
Hill®

ISBN-13: 978-0-373-81512-8

COWBOY DADDY

Copyright © 2010 by Carolyne Aarsen

www.SteepleHill.com

Printed in U.S.A.

Come to me, all you who are weary and burdened,
and I will give you rest.
—*Matthew* 11: 28

To Elin and Annely, who have brought a new
dimension of love to our lives.

Chapter One

What in the world was this about?

"Housekeeper wanted." The words were handwritten, and the notice was tacked up on the bulletin board in Millarville's post office.

Kip Cosgrove ripped the notice down and glared at it, recognizing his younger sister's handwriting. What was Isabelle doing? Where did she get the idea that he needed a housekeeper?

Kip crumpled the paper and threw it in the garbage can of the post office, hoping not too many people had read it.

He spun around, almost bumping into an older woman.

"Hey, Kip, how's your mom?" she asked. "I read on the church bulletin that she had knee surgery."

"She's in a lot of pain," Kip said with a vague smile, taking another step toward the door. He didn't have time for Millarville chitchat. Not with two rambunctious five-year-old boys waiting for him in his truck parked outside the door and a sister to bawl out. "I'll tell her you said hello."

He tipped his cowboy hat, then jogged over to his truck. He had to get home before anyone responded to the advertisement.

"What's the matter, Uncle Kip?"

"Are you mad?"

Justin and Tristan leaned over the front seat of the truck, their faces showing the remnants of the Popsicles he'd given them as a bribe to be quiet on the long trip back from Calgary.

"Buckle up again, you guys," was all he said. He started up the truck, too many things running through his head. Besides looking after his mom and his rebellious younger sister, he had a tractor to fix, hay to haul, horses' hooves to trim and cows to move. And that was today's to-do list.

He managed to ignore the boys tussling in the backseat as he headed down the road, lists and things crowding into his head. Maybe his sister wasn't so wrong in thinking they needed a house-keeper. Even just someone to watch the boys.

No, he reminded himself. Isabelle could do that.

He hunched his shoulders, planning his "you're sixteen-years-old and you can help out over the summer" lecture that he'd already had with his sister once before. Now he had to do it again.

The road made a long, slow bend, and as it straightened, he sighed. The land eased away from the road, green fields giving way to rolling hills. Peaks of granite dusted with snow thrust up behind them, starkly beautiful against the warm blue of the endless sky.

The Rocky Mountains of Southern Alberta. His beloved home.

Kip slowed, as he always did, letting the beauty seep into his soul. But only for a couple of seconds, as a scream from the back pushed his foot a little farther down on the accelerator.

"Justin, go sit down." Kip shot his nephew another warning glance as he turned onto the ranch's driveway.

"Someone is here," Justin yelled, falling over the front seat almost kicking Kip in the face with his cowboy boots, spreading dirt all over the front seat.

Kip pulled to a stop beside an unfamiliar small car. It didn't belong to his other sister, Doreen, that much he knew. Doreen and her husband, Alex, had gone with a full-size van for their brood of eight.

Probably one of his mother's many friends had come to visit. Then his teeth clenched when he noticed that the farm truck was missing, which meant Isabelle was gone. Which also meant she hadn't cleaned the house like he'd told her to.

The boys tumbled out of the truck and Kip headed up the stairs to intercept them before they burst in on his mother's visit. No sense giving the women of Millarville one more thing to gossip about. Kip and those poor, sad little fatherless boys, so out of control. So sad.

Just as he caught their hands, the door of the house opened.

An unfamiliar woman stood framed by the doorway, the late-afternoon sun burnishing her smooth hair, pulled tightly back from a perfectly heart-shaped face. Her porcelain skin, high cheekbones, narrow nose and soft lips gave her an ethereal look at odds with the crisp blue blazer, white shirt and blue dress pants. It was the faintest hint of mystery in her gray-green eyes, however, that caught and held his attention.

What was this beautiful woman doing in his house?

She held up her hands as if to appease him. "Your sister, Isabelle, invited me in. Said you were looking for a housekeeper?" The husky note in her voice created a curious sense of intimacy.

Kip groaned inwardly. He'd taken down the notice too late. "And you are?"

"My name is Nicole."

"Kip Cosgrove." He held out his hand. Her

handshake was firm, which gave him a bit more confidence.

"I'm sorry about coming straight into the house," she said, "but like I said, your sister invited me in, and I thought I should help out right away."

She looked away from him to the boys. Her gentle smile for them softened the angles of her face and turned her from attractive to stunning.

He pushed down his reaction. He had to keep his focus.

"So how long have you been here?" Or, in other words, how long had Isabelle been gone?

"A couple of hours. I managed to get the laundry done and I cleaned the house."

In spite of his overall opposition to Isabelle's harebrained scheme, Kip felt a loosening of tension in his shoulders. He and Isabelle had had a big argument about the laundry and housework before he went to Calgary. Now it was done.

He'd had too many things going on lately. His responsibility for the boys, his mother, Isabelle. The ranch seemed to be a distant fourth in his priorities, which made him even more tense.

Maybe the idea of hiring a housekeeper wasn't so far-fetched.

"You realize my mother has had surgery?" he asked, still not sure he wanted a stranger in the house but also fully aware of his sister's shortcomings in the housekeeping department.

"I've already met her." Her smile seemed to underline her lack of objection. "Isabelle gave me some of the particulars."

"Will you be able to come only certain hours, or do you have other obligations?" He still had his reservations, but since she had come all the way here and had done a bunch of work already, he should ask a few questions.

"I'm not married, if that's what you're asking," Nicole said, brushing a wisp of hair back from her face with one graceful motion.

The gold hoops in her ears caught the sun, as did the rings on her manicured hands.

She didn't look like she'd done much housekeeping. His first impression would have pegged her as a fashion model or businesswoman.

But then he'd been wrong about people before. Case in point: his one-time girlfriend, Nancy. The one who took off as soon as she found out he had been named the guardian of his nephews.

Nicole looked back at the boys, who hadn't said a peep since she had appeared in the doorway. "I'm guessing you are Justin and Tristan?" she asked.

The boys, while boisterous and outgoing around family, were invariably shy around strangers, especially since their father, Scott's death. They clung to Kip and leaned against his legs.

"It's really nice to meet you at…meet you."

Nicole crouched down to the boys' level. He caught the scent of lilacs, saw the curve of her cheek as she glanced from one boy to the other. Her hand reached out, as if to touch them, then retreated.

Something about the gesture comforted him. She seemed drawn to the boys, yet gave them space.

"My nephews are five. They'll be going to school this fall." He tightened his grip on the boys' hands. "Though I hate the thought of putting the little guys on the school bus." Why he told her that, he wasn't sure.

"I told Uncle Kip we have to stay home. To help him with the chores," Tristan said.

"I don't know much about farm chores," Nicole said, glancing from one boy to the other. "What kinds of things do you have to do?"

"We have to feed the dog," Tristan offered quietly. "She has puppies."

"You have puppies?" Nicole's eyes grew wide. "That's pretty neat."

"And we have to help with the baby calves," Justin added, as if unwilling to be outdone by his brother. "But we're not allowed to ride the horses anymore." He shot a hopeful glance Kip's way but he ignored it. The boys had been campaigning all summer to ride again, but there was no way he was putting anyone he loved on a horse. Not since Scott's accident.

They were too young and too precious.

"Now all I have to do is figure out which one of you is Tristan and which is Justin." Nicole looked from one to the other, and the tenderness in her smile eased away Kip's second thoughts.

"He's Tristan," Justin said, pointing to his brother. "And I'm Justin. We're twins."

"I see that. So how should I tell you apart?" Nicole asked.

"Justin has a little brown mark on his back. In the shape of a horseshoe," Tristan offered.

"Do you think it was because you were born on a ranch?"

"Wasn't borned on the ranch. I was borned in the hospital in Halifax." He sighed. "My daddy is dead, you know."

"Dead?" Nicole frowned. "What do you mean?"

"He died when he got on Uncle Kip's horse."

Tristan's comment was said in all innocence, but again the guilt associated with his brother's death washed over Kip.

"Your father is dead?" Nicole said, one hand pressed to her chest.

Why did she sound so shocked? Kip wondered.

"He died when the horse he was on flipped over," Justin continued. "But we know he's in heaven with Jesus. I talk to Jesus and tell him what to say to my daddy every night."

"That's…interesting." A faint note of skepticism entered her voice that concerned him.

"We go regularly to church," Kip said by way of brief explanation. "I hope that's not a problem." He wasn't about to get into a theological discussion about what Jesus meant to him. If he decided to hire her, then she'd find out that faith was woven into every aspect of the Cosgroves' life.

Nicole waved her hand as if dismissing his concerns. "No. Of course not."

"And our mommy is gone," Tristan offered, unwilling to let Justin do all the talking. "She just left us one day. All alone with the babysitter."

"Then Daddy rescued us. He was a good daddy," Justin said.

"How do you know your mommy left you?" A faint edge had entered her voice as she glanced up at Kip. "Do you know where their mother is?"

Kip shook his head, wondering why she wanted to know.

The reality was, no one in the Cosgrove family knew where Tricia was or whether she was dead or alive. His brother, Scott, and Tricia had been living in Nova Scotia when Tricia took off without a word six months after the boys were born.

Scott and his sons then moved back to the ranch.

"Do you want to see our dog's puppies?" Justin

tugged his hand free of Kip's and reached out to Nicole.

"Shouldn't you go and say hi to your Gramma?" Nicole asked.

Kip was pleasantly surprised at her consideration, but he also knew the boys would rather be outside.

"They can go." He wanted a few minutes alone with his mother to get her impression of Nicole.

Tristan grabbed Nicole's other hand and before she could lodge a protest the three of them were off.

Kip watched them head down the sidewalk toward the barn, still unsure. Hiring her would give him a break from the constant nagging he did to get Isabelle to help.

He sighed, glancing at his watch. He should go see his mother and then make sure the boys didn't get into any trouble. Then he had to see what he could do about his tractor.

What had she done?

Nicole bit her lip as she looked down at the sticky faces of the two boys looking up at her, jabbering about cows and puppies and Uncle Kip and Auntie Isabelle and other relatives.

She tried to stifle her guilt.

She was no housekeeper. Nor had she come because of an advertisement. Her real reason for coming to the ranch was to see her nephews. Her sister's boys.

That Kip's sister Isabelle assumed she was the housekeeper had been a coincidence she capitalized on.

She clung to the boys' hands as she felt buffeted by a wave of love. Justin. Tristan. Tricia's twins. A remnant of the true Williams family now that Tricia was dead.

When Tricia had stormed out of their lives all those years ago, yelling that she'd never come back, Nicole had hoped her beloved sister would someday return. Nicole had prayed and had clung to this hope for eight years. However, four weeks ago a police officer showed up at the Williamses' home in Rosedale, Toronto, with the news of Tricia's death and crushed that hope.

Three years ago Tricia had been struck by a car while out walking late at night. She had no identification. It wasn't until Tricia's roommate registered her concern for the missing Tricia that the police were able to identify her body. The roommate knew only that Tricia had recently moved to Halifax and when she had earned enough money she planned to head out west. Then Tricia had had her accident.

The years had slipped by. Then, a month ago,

the roommate moved out of her apartment and in the process had found an envelope behind a desk.

Inside the envelope were letters from Tricia to someone named Scott Cosgrove, a man Tricia apparently had been living with after the boys were born. From what Nicole and her father, Brent, understood from the letters, the boys' biological father was dead. Scott, who was just her boyfriend, had somehow taken Tricia's boys away from her while she was in a drug-rehabilitation program.

These letters had been mailed but returned, marked Address Unknown. These envelopes also contained letters to her sons expressing her love for them and how much she missed them. The final paper was a last will and testament addressed to her parents, asking Brent and Norah Williams to be her sons' guardians in case something happened to her.

The roommate brought all this to the police, who were finally able to inform Nicole and her father what had happened to Tricia. It was also the first time Norah and Brent found out about Tricia's sons.

Nicole had done some detective work and had discovered that Scott had moved back to his family's ranch in Alberta. It took little work from there to discover a Cosgrove family in Millarville,

Alberta. Nicole decided to go to the ranch, to talk to Scott about the boys and to see them.

Nicole's father desperately wanted to come along, but his emphysema was especially bad and his doctor discouraged him from taking the trip. So Nicole came alone.

When Nicole came to the ranch house she wasn't sure what she would do or say or if she was on the right track. She just knew she wasn't leaving until she saw the boys for herself.

When Isabelle answered the door, she assumed Nicole was the housekeeper she'd advertised for and left within seconds of her arrival.

What could Nicole do? She couldn't leave Mrs. Cosgrove, who had been sitting in a wheelchair, alone, nor could she tell the poor woman why she was here. So she stayed and cleaned up and helped where she could.

Then Kip came striding up the sidewalk with his long legs, his eyebrows lowered over narrowed grey eyes shadowed by his cowboy hat, his mouth set in grim lines, and fear clutched her midsection.

She was about to come clean.

Then she saw the boys, and she knew beyond a doubt they were Tricia's twins. Everything changed in that moment, but she couldn't tell the Cosgroves who she was. Not yet.

She didn't want her first introduction to the boys to be fraught with conflict. Because as soon as Kip and his mother, Mary, found out her true purpose for being here, there would be antagonism and battles.

"We have our own kittens, too," Justin said, swinging her hand as if he'd known her for all of his five years.

Nicole tightened her grip on the boys' hands, a surprising wave of love and yearning washing over her.

How could Tricia have left these boys? How horrible her life must have been to make that sacrifice? Why couldn't Tricia have asked for her family's help?

It was because of me, Nicole thought. I sent her away.

"There are five of them," Tristan said, his innocent words breaking into the morass of guilt surrounding any memory of Tricia. "One of them died, though. Do you think that kitten is in heaven with my daddy?"

"I think so," Nicole said, hesitantly. She didn't want to destroy their little dreams of heaven or of the man they thought of as their father. But Scott wasn't their father.

As for God? When Tricia left eight years ago, Nicole's faith in God had wavered. When Nicole's adoptive mother died of cancer three years after that, Nicole stopped thinking God cared.

God, if he did exist, was simply a figurehead.

Someone people went to when they didn't know where else to turn and even then a huge disappointment.

"How about we check out the kittens," she said, brushing aside her anger. All that mattered was that she had found the boys.

"I don't want to see the kittens," Justin said with a pout. "I want to see the horses."

"Uncle Kip won't let us," Tristan said, placing his hands on his hips. "You know that."

"We won't go into the corrals." Justin tugged on her hand. "Uncle Kip won't get mad if we just look."

Nicole easily remembered Kip Cosgrove's formidable expression. Best not cross him sooner than she had to. "Maybe another time," she said. "We should go back to the house."

"I want to see the horses." Justin pulled loose and took off.

"Justin, come back here," she called, still holding onto Tristan as Justin disappeared around the barn.

Nicole turned to Tristan. "You stay here, okay?" She spoke firmly so he understood.

Tristan nodded, his blue eyes wide with uncertainty.

"I have to get your brother." She patted him on the shoulder, allowed herself a moment to cup his soft, tender cheek, then turned to get Justin.

Nicole ran around the barn in time to see Justin with his foot on the bottom rail of the corral. She ran over the uneven ground and caught him by the waistband of his blue jeans just as he took another shaky step up.

"I can go up myself," he said, trying to pull free.

"If your uncle said no, then it's no," Nicole said, shifting her grip from his pants to his shirt. No way was she bucking Uncle Kip on this. She needed all her ammunition for a much bigger battle. "So let's go."

"What's going on?" Kip's deep voice, edged with anger, reverberated through the quiet of the afternoon.

Nicole's heart stuttered at the latent fury in his voice.

Still holding on to Justin's arm, she turned to see Kip standing behind her, Tristan beside him.

"Justin, get down from that fence. You and Tristan are to go back to the house right now," Kip said, his tone brooking no argument. "Gramma is waiting for you."

"I want to stay with Nicole. She said I could see the horses with her."

Nicole was about to correct that when Kip spoke again.

"I need to talk to Miss Nicole," he said. "Alone."

His anger seemed extreme for the circumstances. That could mean only one thing. He knew about her momentary deception.

Time to come clean. She had seen the boys and was ready to face him down. She had Tricia's will and the law on her side.

Justin jumped down and scampered around the barn, Tristan close behind.

Kip watched them leave, then walked toward her, his booted feet stirring up little clouds of dust. The utter stillness of the air felt fraught with uncertainty and a feeling of waiting.

He stopped in front of her, crossed his arms over his chest and angled his head to one side.

Fear trembled in her midsection, threaded with a peculiar awareness of him. She pushed her reaction aside and focused on the job she had come here to do.

"We need to talk," he said quietly.

"I know—"

"I've decided to hire you," he said.

This wasn't what she had expected when he came storming around the barn, anger and fury in his eyes.

"I've got a lot going," he said. "And I can't stay on top of everything. I really could use your help."

The appeal in his voice and the confusion of his

expression created an answering flash of sympathy. When she first came into his house, she felt overwhelmed at the mess. When she saw poor Mrs. Cosgrove, trying to fold laundry from her wheelchair, she knew she couldn't walk away.

So she pitched in and started cleaning. Mrs. Cosgrove's gratitude made her momentary subterfuge seem worthwhile.

Now a man who looked like he could eat bullets and spit out the casings was launching an appeal for her help.

He held his hands up in a gesture of surrender. "So tell me what you want to get paid, and we'll see if we can figure something out."

Nicole held his gaze, and when he gave her a half smile, her heart shifted and softened. For a moment, as their eyes held, a tiny crack opened in her defenses, a delicate pining for something missing in her life. As quickly as it came, she sealed it off. Opening herself up to someone would cost too much.

Besides, he was the enemy. The one who stood between her and her beloved sister's boys. When he found out who she was, the warmth in his eyes would freeze.

She took a breath and plunged in.

"You may as well know, I didn't come to apply for the housekeeping position." Nicole spoke quietly, folding her hands in front of her and forcing herself to hold his gaze. "I'm Tricia's adoptive sister. Justin and Tristan's aunt. I've come to take the boys."

Chapter Two

Kip stared at the woman in front of him, her words spinning around his head.

Tricia's sister? Come to take his boys? His brother's sons?

"What are you talking about? What do you mean?" His heart did a slow flip as the implications of what she said registered.

He had come here to offer her a job, and when he saw Justin climbing the fence of the horse corral, he'd lost it. In front of his very attractive prospective employee.

Now, with his heart still pounding from seeing Justin up on the fence, he was sandbagged with this piece of information.

"When were you going to tell me that you weren't applying for the job?" Kip growled, unable to keep his anger tamped down.

"I just did." Nicole raised her chin and looked

at him with her cool gray-green eyes. "I had no intention of fooling anyone."

Kip gave a short laugh. "So how do you figure you're taking the boys? How does that work?"

Nicole pressed her lips together and looked away. "It works because Tricia wrote up a will stating that our parents get custody and now she's...now she's dead."

Kip took a step back, the news hitting him like a blow.

"What? When?" His poor nephews. How was he going to tell them?

Nicole didn't answer right away, and Kip saw the silvery track of a tear on her cheek. She swiped it away with the cuff of her tailored jacket.

"Tricia died about three years ago. We found out a only few weeks ago." Her voice sounded strangled, and for a moment Kip sympathized with her. The first few weeks after his brother Scott died, he could barely function. He went through the motions of work, hoping, praying, he could find his balance again. Hoping, praying the pain in his heart would someday ease. Hoping the guilt that tormented him over his brother's death would someday be gone as well.

His brother had died only six months ago, and they had only recently found out about Tricia. Her pain must be so raw yet...

He pulled his thoughts back to the problem at

hand. "Why did it take so long for you to find out about Tricia's death?" he asked, steeling his own emotions to her sorrow.

"She hadn't told anyone about her family. Apparently she had just come out of a drug-rehab program. Then she was going to find her boys."

"Drug rehab?" Kip's anger returned. "No wonder Scott came back with the boys."

Nicole shot him an angry glance. "According to Tricia's diary and letters, he took them away without her knowledge or permission. Tricia had moved out of the apartment she shared with Scott and had taken the boys with her. She had brought the boys to a friend's place so she could go into rehab. She was in for two weeks, and when she came back to see the boys, Scott had taken them and was gone."

Kip laughed. "Really."

Nicole shot him a frown. "Yes. Really."

"And you believe a drug user?"

Nicole's frown deepened. "I truly believe that after the boys were born, Tricia had changed. I also believe my sister would not willingly abandon her children."

"But she did."

"Scott took them away from a home she had placed them in so she could get her life together." Nicole drew in a quick breath. "Something he had no right to do."

"How do you figure that?" Kip's anger grew. "He was their father."

"According to what Tricia wrote, the boys were born before she moved in with Scott. He wasn't their father."

Disbelief and anger battled with each other. "That I refuse to believe," he barked. "My brother loved those boys. They are his. You can't prove otherwise. Your sister is a liar."

Nicole's eyes narrowed, and Kip knew he had stepped over a line. He didn't care. This woman waltzes into their lives with this complicated lie and he's supposed to be polite and swallow it all? And then let her take the boys away?

Over his dead body.

"So how do you want to proceed on this?" Nicole asked, arching one perfectly plucked eyebrow in his direction.

Kip mentally heaved a sigh. For a small moment he'd thought this woman was the solution to part of his problems.

Not only was he was back to where he started, even if she was lying, he now had a whole new legal tangle to deal with.

Dear Lord, I don't need anything else right now. I don't have the strength.

He held her steady gaze, determined not to be swayed by the sparkling in her eyes that he suspected were tears. "The boys were left with me as per my brother's verbal request," he said. "I'm their guardian, and until I am notified otherwise, they're not going anywhere and you're not to come back here."

He turned and walked away from the corral. The corral that brought back too many painful memories.

Well, add one more to the list. Somehow he had to tell his nephews that their mother, who had always been a shadowy figure in their lives, was officially dead. If he could believe what this Nicole woman had told him then he had to tell his mother that the woman they had thought was their salvation was anything but.

He shot a quick glance behind him.

Nicole stood by the corral fences, her head bent and her arms crossed over her midsection. Dusty fragments of sunlight gilded her hair and in the silence he heard a muffled sob.

Sympathy for her knotted his chest. Regardless of what he felt, she'd found out about her sister's death only a few weeks ago. Not long enough for the pain to lose that jagged edge. Not near long enough to finish shedding the tears that needed to spill.

For a moment he thought he should go over to her side and offer her what comfort he could. Then he stopped himself.

She wants to take the boys away, he reminded

himself. She claimed they weren't his nephews. And that reminder effectively doused his sympathy.

"I'm sorry, Nicole, but I'd like you to leave," he said, hoping his voice projected a tiny bit of sympathy.

She drew in a shuddering breath and looked up, a streak of mascara marring her ethereal features.

"I have pictures," she said.

"What is that supposed to mean?"

"It means I can prove who I am." Nicole wiped at her cheeks with the tips of her fingers, a delicate motion belying the strength of conviction in her voice. "I also have a signed letter from my sister along with a copy of her last will and testament." Nicole took a few steps toward him, wrapping her arms around her waist. "So I'm not without ammunition myself."

"I'd like to see all that."

"Fine." She walked past him, the scent of lilacs trailing behind her.

Kip followed her as regret lingered a moment.

She was a beautiful woman. When he still thought of her as his future housekeeper, he had thought having her around every day might have been a distraction. He was lonely, she was beautiful. Maybe not the best mix.

But now?

Right now she was a complication he didn't know how to work his way around.

She yanked a key ring out of her coat pocket, pointed it at the car and unlocked the door. Ducking inside, she pulled out a briefcase, which she set on the trunk of the car.

Kip came closer as she drew an envelope out of the case, opened it and took out a picture.

"This is my sister, the boys and your brother. I think the boys are about six months old there."

Kip took the laminated photo, and as he glanced at it he felt as if spiders scuttled across his gut.

The picture was identical to one he'd had blown up, then framed and hung in the boy's room. The only picture the boys had of their mother.

As he handed the picture back, sorrow mixed with his anger. Two of the people in the picture were dead. The boys were officially orphans.

Nicole tucked her hair behind her ears, tugged on her jacket and looked him in the eye. "I'm leaving your ranch like you asked me, but I'm not going far. I have a room in a motel in Millarville and I intend on coming here every day to see my nephews."

"I'm not discussing anything to do with the boys without my lawyer present. So until then, as I said before, I'd like you to stay away."

She looked like she was about to protest, then gave a delicate shrug. "Fine. When do you want to see your lawyer?"

Never. He had cows to move to other pastures.

A tractor to fix, a stock waterer to repair and a sister who would be peeved when she discovered they didn't have a housekeeper after all.

"Tomorrow," he said, mentally cringing. He'd just have to work later in the evening to make up for lost time. Hopefully he could get in with Ron, his lawyer. If not, well, she'd have to wait.

"What's his name and number?" She pulled out a phone, then punched in the information he gave her. "And what time?" she asked, looking up.

"I'll give you a call." He wondered what Ron would have to say about the situation.

Nicole put the phone away, then reached into a side pocket of the briefcase she had taken the papers from.

She pulled out a business card and handed it to him.

He glanced down at the name embossed on the card.

Nicole Williams. Director, Williams Foundation. The information was followed by several numbers—home, office, fax, cell—and an email address and a website.

Very official and a bit intimidating.

"Director of the Williams Foundation?" he asked, flicking the card between his fingers.

"My adoptive parents started it."

"Adoptive?"

"Brent and Norah Williams adopted me when

I was eight," Nicole said, her voice matter of fact. "My father started the nonprofit in memory of my adoptive mother."

"Admirable." He tucked the card in the back pocket of his worn jeans, hoping this wasn't the pair with the hole in the pocket. "I'll let you know what's up."

"Can I come tomorrow to see the boys?"

"Let's wait to see what my lawyer says."

Nicole squeezed the top of her briefcase, averting her eyes. "They're my nephews too," she said quietly. "My sister's boys."

"Boys she abandoned, that no one bothered to find."

Nicole's eyes grew hard. "They were taken away from her. The lack of communication is hardly my fault considering we found out about these boys only a few weeks ago."

Kip was about to say something more when a truck turning onto the yard caught his attention. Isabelle.

His younger sister pulled up beside Nicole's car, putting it between her and her brother. A strategic move he thought, fighting his anger and frustration with her.

"Hey, **Nicole**. How'd things go today?" Isabelle called out as she jumped out of the truck. "Had to get groceries," she said to Kip holding up a solitary plastic bag as if to underline her defense.

"Dressed like that?" Kip asked, eyeing her bright red lipstick, snug T-shirt that sparkled in the sunlight and her too-tight blue jeans.

Isabelle's face grew mutinous. "I didn't think I had to stick around here. Especially since Nicole showed up." She pulled another bag out of the truck and flounced up the walk to the house, her dark hair bouncing with every step.

Kip bit back whatever he wanted to say to his little sister, fully aware of his audience.

Too many things going on, he thought, fighting his frustration with his sister and this new, huge complication.

"I'm going now," Nicole said, her voice quiet, well modulated. She gave him a tight smile, then pulled her briefcase off the trunk of the car. "I'll wait to hear from you."

Without a second glance, she got in, started the engine and roared away from him in a cloud of dust.

Kip pushed back his hat as he watched her leave, frustration clawing at him.

Please Lord, don't let my family be broken up, he prayed. *Don't let her take my boys away from me.*

And please don't let me lose it with my sister.

He stepped into the house just as his mother wheeled herself into the kitchen. Her long, graying hair was brushed and neatly swept up into a ponytail, her brown eyes sparkled, and the smile on her face was a welcome respite from the resignation that had been his mother's default expression since her surgery.

"Where did Nicole go?" his mother asked, sounding happier than she had in a while. "She seems like a lovely girl. I'm looking forward to having her around to help out."

Kip glanced at the clean countertop and shining sink. When he first saw how clean the house was he couldn't believe that businesslike woman had done all this. Now he knew she was simply trying to weasel her way into his mother's good graces.

"Where's Isabelle?"

"In her room."

"When did she leave the ranch?"

Mary Cosgrove tapped her finger against her lips. "About one."

Three hours to pick up one bag of groceries. He was so going to talk to his little sister. Leaving his mother alone with a stranger, even if she had come here because of an advertisement, was irresponsible.

Not only a stranger, a woman who had come to completely disrupt their lives.

"I'm so glad you decided to take on a housekeeper," his mother continued, sounding hopeful. "She seems so capable and organized."

Kip hated to burst her bubble. "I still think

Isabelle should learn to pull her share of the housework."

His mother sighed. "I know, and I agree, but it's so much work to get her motivated and Nicole seems so capable." Mary looked past Kip. "Where is Nicole now?"

"She left." Kip blew out his breath and dropped into a chair across from her mother. "Truth is, she didn't come for the housekeeping job. She came..." he hesitated, glancing up at his mother, who seemed more relaxed than she had in months. Scott's death had been devastating for her. This new piece of information wouldn't help. "Nicole, apparently, is Tricia's sister."

His mother frowned. "Tricia? Scott's girl-friend?"

"Yep. The mother of the boys."

Mary's fingers fluttered over her heart, her eyes wide in a suddenly pale face. "What did she want?"

Kip wrapped his rough hands around his mother's cold ones. "She claims she has a will granting her custody of Justin and Tristan."

"But the boys' mother...Tricia..." Mary squeezed her son's hands. "Where is she?"

"She's dead." The words sounded harsh, even though he'd never met the woman. But she had been the mother of his nephews.

The nephews that Nicole claimed didn't belong

to Kip's family. Kip's heart turned over in his chest.

There was no way he was telling his mother that piece of information. He didn't believe that fact for one minute anyhow. Scott had loved those boys. Doted on them.

Since Scott died, Kip had fought to keep this family together, but lately he felt as if everything he worked so hard for was slipping out of his fingers.

There was no way he was letting Nicole take his mother's only connection to Scott away. No way.

Chapter Three

"I found them. I found the boys." Nicole tucked the phone under her chin as she sorted through her clothes. The motel room held a small dresser and minuscule closet she could hang some clothes in. She had packed a variety of clothes, unsure what she would need.

She closed the closet door and glanced around the room. It was the best, supposedly, in Millarville, and she guessed it would do. She hoped she wouldn't have to stay here long. Staying here resurrected memories she had relegated to the "before" part of her life.

Before the Williams family took her in.

"Are they okay? How do they look?" Her father sounded a bit better, as if the news sparked new life in him.

"They're fine." Nicole thought of Justin and Tristan, and her heart contracted.

She knew the Cosgroves wouldn't simply hand over the boys to her as soon as she had arrived. From what she had discovered, the boys had been at the ranch since Scott took them away.

Kip's family was the only one the children knew. A family, she discovered, which included Kip's mother, a younger sister and a married sister with six children.

Nicole couldn't stop a nudge of jealousy at the thought of Kip's large family, then quashed it. She'd had a full life with the Williams, and she owed her adoptive parents more than she could ever repay. That Brent's natural daughter was the one gone only increased her guilt.

"Is the family treating them okay? Do they seem to have a stable home life?"

"The farmhouse is a bit of a wreck," Nicole said, thinking of the worn flooring, and the faded paint. "It looks as if no money had been spent on the house in a while."

Yet in spite of the mess, when she walked into the spacious kitchen of the Cosgrove house, she felt enveloped by a sense of home. Of comfort and peace.

Something she seldom experienced in her father's cavernous house.

"They're well taken care of." She tucked the phone under her ear, pulled her laptop out of the bag and plugged it in. Thankfully, she would be able to do much of her work for the family's foundation while she was here.

"You sound like you think they should stay." Her father's voice held an accusatory tone.

"No. I don't," Nicole assured him. "But we can't simply remove them immediately." She knew she sounded practical, however, her feelings were anything but.

When she saw the boys, a feeling of love, almost devastating in its intensity, bowled her over. She wanted to grab them, hold them close, then run away with them. She couldn't understand or explain the unexpected power of these feelings. The only time she'd experienced this before was when she saw her little sister, Tricia, for the first time.

"It was what your sister wanted," her father said, a hard note entering his voice.

"I know. It's what I want as well, but we have to proceed carefully. The boys don't remember their mother and they most certainly don't know who I am." She highly doubted Kip would tell them in the next few days.

"I should be there," her father said, his voice harsh. "I should be meeting with that lawyer." This was followed by a bout of coughing that belied his insistence.

"You know yourself that once lawyers get hold of things, the process grinds to a halt." She ignored a sliver of panic at the thought. When she arranged to come here, she had given herself three weeks to bring the boys back. Sure, she could work here, but she also needed to spend time with the boys so the transition from here to Toronto wouldn't be so difficult.

"Who do the boys look like?" Brent asked, a thread of hope in his voice.

"They look exactly like Tricia." Nicole pressed her fingers to her lips, restraining her sorrow.

"You have to bring my boys back, Nicole. They are all I have left of Tricia. Those boys don't belong there. They're not even blood relatives."

Nicole knew her father spoke out of sorrow, but his words struck at the foundations of Nicole's insecurities. Tricia was Sam and Norah's natural daughter.

Nicole was simply the adopted one.

"Tomorrow I'll see Mr. Cosgrove's lawyer," Nicole said, opening her laptop and turning it on. "We'll have to take this one step at a time."

"When you talk to that lawyer you make sure to let him know that James Feschuk is working for us. His reputation might get things moving a bit. I also want a DNA test. If they don't believe us, then we'll get positive proof that Scott Cosgrove was not the boys' father."

"How will that happen?" Nicole asked.

"James told me that you can get DNA tests done locally. He suggested one called a grandparent's test. Get that grandmother to get tested and we'll find out. I'll get tested too. Then we've got some teeth to our argument." His voice rose and Sam started coughing again.

"I'm saying goodbye," Nicole said. "And you should go to bed. Make sure you take your medication and use that puffer the doctor gave you."

"Yes, yes," Sam said. "I'll get James to phone that lawyer. Tell him we insist on a DNA test. Give me his name and I can take care of it."

Nicole pulled out her cell phone and called up the name and number and gave that information to her father. "I'll let you know the minute I hear anything."

Nicole said goodbye. She turned back to her computer, but only sat and stared sightlessly at the screen, her work suddenly forgotten as she thought of Justin and Tristan. Tricia's boys.

Seeing them had been heartwarming and heart-rending at the same time.

Again she felt the sting of her sister's betrayal when Tricia had left without a word those many years ago. Nicole had hoped and prayed for an opportunity to talk to her face-to-face, to apologize. But the only letter in the envelope was one to her parents pleading for forgiveness. Nothing for her.

Nicole glanced around the room as memories of other evenings in other motel rooms crowded in.

Nicole tried to push the memories away, but the emotions of the past day had made her vulnerable and her mind slipped back to a vivid picture of herself, sitting on a bed in a motel room, a little girl of five, waiting while her aunt smoked and strode back and forth, watching through the window.

When Nicole's natural mother died, her father, a long-distance trucker, put Nicole into the care of his sister, a bitter, verbally abusive woman.

Whenever he came into town, Nicole's aunt would bring her to a motel where they would meet her father. She would stay with him for a couple of days and then he would be gone.

That evening they waited until the next morning, but he never came. His truck had spun out of control and he had died in the subsequent accident.

After six months, her aunt had her moved to an already-full foster home.

Four years later, she was adopted by the Williams family at age eight, and her life went from the instability of seven foster homes in four years to the stability of a wealthy family. She was told enough times how blessed she was, and she knew it.

Yet each night as she crawled into her bed, she would wonder when it would all get taken away. People had always left her. It would happen again.

Then something magical and miraculous happened to her and the Williams family. Norah, who was never supposed to be able to conceive, became pregnant. When Tricia was born, Nicole bonded with this little baby in a way she couldn't seem to with Norah and Sam. Tricia became as much Nicole's child as her parents'.

Nicole took care of her with a fierce intensity. She stood up for her in school, listened to her stories of heartbreak and sorrow. Defended her to Sam and Norah whenever Tricia got into yet another scrape. She was Tricia's confidant.

Then Tricia turned thirteen. She withdrew. Became sullen and ungrateful. She started hanging around with the wrong crowd and staying out late. Nicole had tried to reason with her, to explain that she was throwing her life away.

But Tricia kept up her self-destructive lifestyle. Finally, in frustration, Nicole fought with her.

Then Tricia, too, left and never came back.

Nicole got up, grabbed her purse and walked out of the motel. She walked down the street, then up it again. She let the cooling mountain air soothe away the memories. She bought a sandwich, returned to her motel room and dove into her work. A few hours later she took a shower and crawled, exhausted, into bed. She needed all the rest could she get.

Tomorrow she would be seeing Kip Cosgrove again.

Tomorrow she would have other battles to fight.

"So she has some legitimacy?" Kip leaned his elbows on his knees, then frowned at the grass stain he saw on his blue jeans. He should have checked before he put the pants on. Of course he was in a hurry when he left the ranch. Of course he had to go through a mini battle to get Isabelle to agree to take care of her nephews while he was gone.

"As an aunt to the boys, she has as much right as you do," Ron Benton, his lawyer, said, leaning his elbows on the desk. "As for her claim about Scott not being the father, unfortunately it's a matter of her word against yours now that both the principals in this case are dead. We'll need more information."

"Tricia abandoned the boys, Ron. She left them with Scott. She was gone for three years."

"Well, now we know she was dead for three years."

Kip blew out a sigh of frustration at that irrefutable truth. When Nicole had told him that, he felt as if his world had been realigned. Ever since Scott showed up at the farm with the two boys, Kip had burned with a righteous indignation that a woman could leave these boys all alone. An indignation that grew with each year of no communication.

Now he found out she'd been dead and possibly didn't know where Scott was.

If what Nicole said was true.

"The trouble is we don't have a legal document that grants custody to you," Ron said. "And it sounds like this Nicole might have one that gives it to her. Though you've been the primary care-giver—and any court would look at that as well— the reality is you don't have legal backup for your case. As well, we don't know why Tricia left."

"I know what Scott told me."

Ron blew his breath out, tapping his fingers against the sleeve of his suit jacket. "She and Scott got along? He never did anything to her?"

"Of course not." Kip barked his reply, then forced himself to settle down. Ever since Nicole had walked into their lives, he'd been edgy and distracted.

He had too much responsibility. The words dropped into his mind with the weight of rocks.

How could he think that? He loved his nephews dearly. He wasn't going to let Nicole take them away. Especially not after promising his dying brother that he would take care of them. There was no way he was backing out on that. Not after what had happened to Scott.

Guilt over his brother's death stabbed him again. If only he hadn't let him get on that horse. The horse was too green, he had told him, but Scott was insistent. Kip should have held his ground.

Should have. He shoved his hand through his hair. The words would haunt him for the rest of his life.

"Trouble is, we don't have a lot to go on," Ron continued. "Your main weapon is the primary-caregiver option. You've been taking care of Justin and Tristan. That's what we'll have to go with if this gets to court."

"Court? Would it get that far?"

Ron lifted his shoulder in a shrug. "I'll have to do some digging to see if I can avoid that, but no promises."

No time. No time.

The words bounced around Kip's mind, mocking him. He didn't have time to fight this woman.

"Whatever happens, I'm not letting some high and mighty Easterner come and take the boys simply because she has some piece of paper and I don't," Kip said as the door to the office opened.

He stopped mid rant and turned in his chair in time to see Nicole standing in the doorway, the overhead lights of the office glinting off her long, blond hair and turning her gray-green eyes into chips of ice.

overhead lights of the office, filling the office...
about hair and turning her gaze across to the...
ripple of see

Chapter Four

Nicole glared at Kip Cosgrove, wondering if he could read the anger in her eyes. She doubted it. He sat back in the chair, looking as if he was completely in charge of the situation and his world.

I've got a legal will, she reminded herself.

The boys are Tricia's.

"Good morning," she said, projecting pleasant briskness into her voice. She'd dressed with care this morning. Her tailored suit was her defense in the boardroom of her father's foundation and it became her armor now.

Her gaze ticked over Kip and moved to the man sitting on the other side of the desk. He certainly didn't look like any lawyer she had ever met with his open-necked twill shirt, blue jeans and cowboy boots. She was definitely not in Toronto anymore. "My name is Nicole Williams, but I'm sure you already know that."

"Ron Benton." He stood, gave her a slow-release grin and shook her hand. At least he looked friendly, which was more than she could saw for Kip Cosgrove with his deep scowl.

Ron sat back in his chair, his arms crossed over his chest. "I understand we have a problem that we need to resolve."

Nicole shrugged as she set her briefcase on the floor beside her chair. "No problem as far as I can see. I have a will from Tricia Williams giving her parents, Sam and Norah Williams, full custody of the boys, Justin and Tristan Williams. Norah Williams has passed away, but Sam is very much alive." Nicole took out a copy of the will and placed it on the wooden desk in front of Ron. "You can keep that for your records."

Ron glanced over the papers. "This will hasn't been filed with any legal firm, or put together with the help of a lawyer?"

Nicole shook her head. "No, but it is witnessed and dated."

"By whom?" Ron kept his eyes on the papers, flipping through them as he frowned.

"I don't know the woman. Apparently it was someone that Tricia lived with."

Ron's slow nod combined with his laissez-faire attitude grated on Nicole, but she kept her temper in check. She had to stay in control.

Then Ron sat back in his chair, his hands laced

behind his head. "We could easily contest the legality of this will."

Now it was Nicole's turn to frown. "What do you mean?"

"How do we know this is Tricia William's signature? And who was this friend? Anyone could have put this together."

Kip leaned forward and she couldn't help glancing his way, catching a gleam in his eye.

"So you're saying this isn't as cut-and-dried as some people think?" Kip asked.

Hard not to miss the pleasure in his voice. Nicole fought back her concern. She had too much riding on this situation. Sam was expecting her to bring these boys back. It was what she had to do.

"Unfortunately, no."

"So that makes things a bit easier," Kip said with an obvious note of relief in his voice.

"We have our own lawyer working on this case," Nicole added, just in case Kip thought she was simply rolling over. "We have copies of Tricia's handwriting and photographs of the boys."

"Birth certificates?" Ron asked, his chair creaking as he leaned forward, glancing over the will again.

Nicole had to say no. "Again, that's something our lawyer, James Feschuk is working on." Dropping James's name, however, got no reaction.

"So things are still in limbo?" Kip asked. He

tapped a booted foot on the carpet, as if he couldn't wait to get out of there. Nicole wasn't surprised.

He looked as if he was far more at home on the back of a horse than sitting in an office.

Which made her wonder why he wouldn't let the boys on the horses. He seemed so unreasonably angry with her when she took them to the horse corrals.

And why did she care? The boys were leaving this life as soon as possible.

Ron tapped his fingers on the desk, shaking his head as if to negate everything Nicole had said. "I'm sorry, but I don't think anything can happen until we get all our questions answered."

"Great." Kip got to his feet. "Then we'll wait."

"Not so fast, Kip," Ron continued. "The other reality is we can't completely negate Ms. Williams's claim on these boys. She does have some rights for now."

Nicole's frustration eased off. She had been ready to do battle with this small-town lawyer.

Kip had already grabbed his denim jacket but clutched it now, his grey eyes staying on Ron, ignoring Nicole. "What rights?"

"Visitation, for one," Ron said.

Kip blew out a sigh and shoved his hands through his hair as he glared at his own lawyer. "How will that work?"

Time to take control. "I would like to visit the boys every day," Nicole said.

Kip finally turned his attention to her. "Every day? For how long?"

"I think that's something we can settle here and now," Nicole said. "I was thinking I could come and pick up the boys and take them for a visit either morning or afternoon. Whichever is convenient."

Kip made a show of looking at his watch, as if he was the only one in this room with a schedule to keep. Then he sat down and leaned back in his chair. "Okay, I'm thinking something else. I'm thinking you can see the boys every day, but the visits have to happen on the ranch and under my supervision."

Nicole frowned at that. "Why?"

Kip held her gaze, his frown and piercing gaze giving him a slightly menacing air. "I only have your word that you are who you are, and until Ron is satisfied, I'm not letting Justin and Tristan out of my sight."

His antagonism was like a wave and for the briefest moment, fear flashed through Nicole. He reminded her of a wolf, defending its pups.

Then she pushed her fear down.

"And how would these visits be apportioned?"

"I'm guessing you mean how much time and when?"

"Precisely."

Kip raised an eyebrow and Nicole knew she was putting on her "office" voice. She couldn't help it. She felt as if she needed the defense.

"You come from 2:30 until 5:00 every afternoon. That's what works best for me."

She bit back her anger. Two and a half hours? Was that what he considered a visit?

"Take it or leave it," he added.

She didn't have much choice. Right now she may hold a legal will, but until it was proven legitimate, he had the right of possession—if that was the correct way to term guardianship of the boys.

"Those terms are…fine with me," she said, trying to sound reasonable. She wasn't fighting him over this. Not yet. In the end, she knew she would be proven right, but in the meantime the boys were in his care and on his ranch and she could do nothing about that.

"So we should draw something up," Ron said, pulling out a pen. "Just in case there are any repercussions."

Fifteen minutes later, papers were printed up and signed and everyone given a copy.

Kip folded his over and shoved them in the back pocket of his jeans. She put hers in her briefcase.

"There is one more thing," Nicole said quietly. "My father insists that we do a DNA test."

"What?" The word fairly exploded out of

Kip's mouth. "What do you think this is? *CSI Alberta?*"

"It's not that complex. There is a test that can be ordered, and I've checked into the locations of the clinics where they can be brought. We would require your mother to take a test and my father, given that the parents of the boys are dead."

"Is this legal?" Kip asked his lawyer.

Ron leaned back in his chair, tapping his pen against his chin. "Might not be a bad idea. It could bolster your case, Kip."

More likely ours, Nicole thought.

Kip narrowed his eyes as he looked at Nicole, as if he didn't trust her. "Okay. If you think it will help, Ron, I'll get Mom to do it."

"I'll find out more about it and let you know what has to happen," Ron said.

"So that's settled." Kip shrugged his jacket on and gave Nicole the briefest of nods. "I'll see you tomorrow."

Nicole gave him a crisp smile. "Actually, I'd like to come now."

Kip faltered, his frown deepening. "As in today?"

"As in, I have just been granted visitation from 2:30 to 5:00 every afternoon." Nicole gave him a cool look as she too got to her feet. She didn't like him towering over her, but even in her heels, she only reached his shoulder.

"I thought we'd start tomorrow."

"I have every right to start today." She had signed a paper giving her those rights. He had no reason to deny her.

Kip blew out a sigh as he dropped a tattered cowboy hat on his head. "I don't have time today."

Nicole lifted her shoulder in a delicate shrug. "You're the one who set out the terms of the visits."

Kip held her gaze, his eyes shadowed by the brim of the cowboy hat. Then he glanced down at her tailored suit and laughed. "Okay, but you'd better change. The boys are helping me fix a tractor this afternoon."

"Should I bring a hammer?" she said, determined not to let him goad her.

"Just a three-eighth-inch wrench and a five-sixteenth-inch socket," he returned.

"Excellent. I just happened to bring mine along."

"In your Louis Vuitton luggage?" This was tossed back at her underlined with the arching of one of his eyebrows.

"No. Coach." And how would a cowboy like him know about Louis Vuitton?

"Cute." He buttoned his jacket. "This has been fun, but I've got work to do," he said in a tone that implied "fun" was the last thing he'd been having. "See you when we see you."

When he closed the door behind him, it was as if the office deflated. Became less full, less dynamic.

Nicole brushed the feeling off and turned to Ron. "I'll get my lawyer to call you. He'll bring you up to speed on his side of the case, and the two of you can discuss the DNA tests."

Ron got to his feet and pursed his lips. Then he sighed. "I'm not speaking as a lawyer anymore, but as a friend of Kip's. You may as well know that Kip Cosgrove dotes on those boys. He goes everywhere with them. Does everything with them. He has since those boys moved to the ranch with his brother."

"They're not even his." As soon as Nicole spoke the words she regretted giving her thoughts voice. She knew how coldhearted that must have sounded to Ron.

The reality was she knew firsthand what it was like to be the one pushed aside. She had been in enough homes as the "outsider," the nonbiological child, to know that no matter what, biology always won out. The "natural" children were always treated differently than the "foster" child.

Ron shot her an angry look. "That is the last thing on Kip's mind," he snapped. "Those boys have been in his life since they were one year old. Living on the ranch is the only life they know."

Nicole held his angry gaze, determined not to let his opinion of her matter. "They only know this life because Scott took them away from their biological mother." She picked up her briefcase and slung her trench coat over her arm. "Now all I need to know is where I can buy some tools."

This netted her a puzzled look from Ron. "Why?"

"Because I fully intend on helping fix that tractor."

Chapter Five

Kip pulled off his "town" shirt and tossed it onto his unmade bed. He grabbed the work shirt from the floor where he'd tossed it. He'd been in too much of a rush to clean up before he left for town.

He buttoned up his shirt as he headed down the stairs to where the boys were playing a board game at the kitchen table with his mom.

Isabelle stood at the kitchen sink, washing dishes from lunch, her expression letting him know exactly what she thought of this chore.

"Oh, Gramma, you have to go down the snake," Justin shouted, waving his arms in the air as if he had won the Stanley Cup.

"Oh dear, here I go," Kip's mother said, reaching across the board to do as Justin said. "This puts me way behind."

Kip caught her grimace as she sat back in

her wheelchair and wondered again how long it would be before his mother was mobile. Though the kitchen was still clean from Nicole's visit on Saturday, he knew it was simply a matter of time before things slowly deteriorated.

"Isabelle, that laundry that got folded yesterday is still in the laundry basket upstairs," Kip said.

"Yeah. I know."

"So what should happen with it?"

Isabelle set a plate on the drying rack with agonizing slowness, punctuated her movement with a sigh, then shrugged. "I guess I should put it away."

"I guess," he reiterated.

"I think someone is here," Tristan said, standing up on his chair.

Kip groaned. Probably Nicole. Well, she'd have to tag along with him. He had promised the boys they could help him fix the tractor. They weren't much help, but they were slowly learning how to read wrench sizes and knew the difference between a Phillips and a flat screwdriver. Plus, it was a way to spend time with them.

"It's Nicole," Justin yelled, confirming what Kip suspected. "I'm going to go say hi." He jumped off his chair, Tristan right behind him. The porch door slammed shut behind them, creating a momentary quiet in the home.

His mother turned in her wheelchair, wincing

as she did so. "Now that the boys are gone, what did Ron tell you?"

Kip glanced out of the window. Nicole was barely out of her car and the boys were already grabbing her hands. Their hasty switch in allegiances bothered him in a way he didn't want to scrutinize.

Isabelle stopped what she was doing and turned around, listening with avid interest.

"For now we have to allow her visits with the boys," Kip said, rolling up the sleeves of his shirt. "He's looking into how legitimate Tricia's will is, but nothing has been settled And ..." he hesitated, wondering what his mother would think of this new wrinkle. "She and her father insist on you taking a DNA test."

His mother frowned. "Is that hard? Do I have to go to the hospital?"

"Apparently there's a test for grandparents. You can order it and then bring the results to a couple of clinics not far away. It's nothing to worry about. Just a formality so we can prove that Scott is as much a parent to the boys as Tricia was."

Kip stopped there. Until Nicole brought the news she had, Kip hadn't been able to think of Tricia without a surge of anger. She'd left her boys behind. But knowing she had been dead the past years changed a lot.

And raised a few more questions.

Kip brushed them aside. The boys were Scott's. He knew it beyond a doubt. Scott wouldn't have taken them with him back to the ranch if they weren't.

"So Nicole is really the twins' aunt too?" Isabelle asked.

"I think so."

"Is she taking the boys?"

Kip shot Isabelle a warning glance. "No one is taking the boys anywhere. They belong here."

His mother placed her hand on his arm. "But if she's their aunt—"

Kip squeezed his mother's hand in reassurance. "I won't let it happen. I promised Scott I would keep the boys on the ranch, and I keep my promises."

"You always have," Mary Cosgrove said with a wan smile. "You've been a good son. I'm so thankful for you. I still hope and pray that you'll find someone who sees past that gruff exterior of yours and sees you for who you really are." She gave his hands a gentle shake. "Nancy Colbert didn't know what she gave up when she broke up with you."

Kip sighed. He didn't want to think about his ex-girlfriend either. "Nancy was never cut out to be a rancher's wife," he said.

"I never liked that Nancy chick," Isabelle added. "She reminded me of a snake."

"Thanks for that, Izzy. Maybe those dishes could get done before the day is over."

This piece of advice netted him an eye roll, but she turned back to the sink and plodded on.

"I still wonder, if you hadn't agreed to take on the boys, if she would have stayed with you..." his mother's voice trailed off, putting voice to the questions that had plagued Kip for the first two months after Scott had died.

"Scott begged me, Mom," Kip reminded her. "He begged me to keep the boys on the ranch. I owed him. It was because of my horse—" he stopped himself there. He still couldn't think of his brother's death without guilt. He wondered if that would ever leave. "Besides, if Nancy had really loved me, she would have been willing to take on the boys as well as me."

Mary nodded, but Kip could see a hint of sorrow in her assuring smile.

"I know you really liked her, but the reality is anyone who wants me will have to take the boys and the ranch as well—"

"And your mother and your little sister," Mary added. She shook her head. "You took too much on when you took over the ranch after Dad died. You take too much on all the time."

Kip gave her a quick hug. "I do it because I love you, and anything taken on in love isn't a burden." He heard the noise of the boys' excited voices coming closer. "And now I'd better deal with Ms. Williams."

He gently squeezed his mother's shoulder, squared his own and went out the door.

Nicole was leading the boys up the walk, holding both boys' hands. She looked up at him and Kip felt a jolt of surprise.

She had completely transformed. Gone was the suit, the tied-back hair, the high-heeled shoes. The uptight city woman had been transformed.

She wore blue jeans, a loose plaid shirt over a black T-shirt and cowboy boots. And she had let her hair down. It flowed over her shoulders in loose waves, softening her features.

Making her look more approachable and, even worse, more appealing.

He put a brake on his thoughts, blaming his distraction on his mother's mention of his old girlfriend. Though he didn't miss Nancy as much as he'd thought he would, there were times he missed having someone special in his life. Missed being a boyfriend. He'd always wanted a family of his own.

"Hello," Nicole said, her voice as cool as it had been in Ron's office.

He acknowledged her greeting with a curt nod. "Okay boys, let's go work on that tractor."

"Yippee." Justin jumped up and down. "Let's go, Tristan."

Kip glanced at his other nephew who was staring up at Nicole, looking a little starstruck. "I want to play with the puppies," Tristan said. "Can you play with the puppies with me?" he asked Nicole.

"I thought you wanted to help me," Kip said to Tristan with a forced jocularity. Tristan was never as adventurous as Justin, but he always came along.

Tristan shook his head still looking up at Nicole. "I want to be with Auntie Nicole."

Auntie Nicole? The words jarred him, and he stifled a shiver of premonition. She had already staked a claim on his boys.

"So do I," Justin shouted out.

Nicole glanced from Kip to the boys. "Your Uncle Kip said I had to help him with the tractor." She shot him an arch look. "Unless he was kidding."

"Nope," he said, deadpan. "Absolutely serious."

"Then I'll come," Justin said, turning on his allegiances as quickly as he turned on his feet.

"What are those," Nicole asked, as they walked past two of his wagons parked beside the barn. Grass had grown up a bit around them. He'd parked them there last fall and hadn't touched them since.

"Chuck wagons."

"What do you use them for?" Nicole asked.

"Uncle Kip used to race them," Tristan said. "Before my daddy died."

"Race them? How do you do that?"

"You don't know?" Justin's astonishment was a bit rude, but Kip didn't feel like correcting him.

"I'm sorry. I do not."

Kip wasn't surprised. Chuck-wagon racing had originated in Calgary, and while it was an integral part of the Calgary Stampede, it wasn't a regular event in all the rodeos scattered around North America. He'd grown up with it, though. His father and his uncle and his grandfather all competed in the chuck-wagon races. It was in his blood.

He knew he should be teaching the boys so they could carry on the tradition. It was in their blood too. They were as much Cosgroves as he was.

"Uncle Kip will have to show you, won't you, Uncle Kip?" Justin said.

"Maybe," was his curt reply.

Since Scott died, he hadn't worked with his horses. Hadn't competed in any of the races. Chuck-wagon racing took up too much of the time he didn't have anymore.

He felt a pinch of sorrow. He missed the thrill of the race, the keenness of competing, the pleasure of working with his horses.

"Uncle Kip was one of the fastest racers," Tristan said, pride tingeing his voice. "But he doesn't race anymore. He says it's not 'sponsible 'cause now he has us."

"Well, that sounds like a good way to think," Nicole said.

Kip shot her a glance, wondering if she was serious. But he caught her steady gaze and she wasn't laughing.

"So where's the tractor?"

"Just over here." He was only too glad to change the subject. Chuck wagons were in his past. He had enough going on in the present.

"What do we need to do?" Nicole asked as they walked across the packed ground toward the shop.

Kip gave her a curious look. "You don't have to help."

"Of course I do." She gave him a wry look, as if to say "you asked for it."

Their eyes held a split-second longer than necessary. As if each was testing the other to see who would give. Then he broke the connection. He didn't have anything to prove.

Yet even as he thought those brave words, a finger of fear trickled down his spine. Actually, he did have something to prove. He had to prove that Justin and Tristan's were Scott's boys. That they belonged here on the ranch.

Kip pulled on the chain and the large garage door creaked and groaned as light spilled into the usually gloomy shop. He loved working with the door open and today, with the sun shining and a bright blue sky, was a perfect day to do so.

"This is where the tractor is," Justin said. "Uncle Kip took it apart and he said a bad word when he dropped a wrench on his toe."

"Did he now?" Nicole's voice held a hint of laughter and Kip made a mental note to talk to the boys about "things we don't tell Ms. Williams."

"Tristan, you can wheel over the tool chest. Justin, you can get me the box of rags," Kip said, shooting his blabbermouth nephew a warning look as he rolled up his sleeves.

"I got the rags the last time," Justin whined. "How come Tristan always gets to push the tool chest? I never do."

As Kip stifled his frustration, he caught Nicole watching him. As if assessing what he was going to do.

"Just do it, Justin," he said more firmly.

But Justin shoved his hands in his pockets and glared back at him. Kip felt Nicole's gaze burning on him. For a moment he wished he hadn't insisted that she visit the kids here. Now everything he did with the boys would be with an audience. A very critical audience who, he was sure, would be only too glad to see him mess up.

He tried to ignore her presence as he knelt down in front of Justin. "Buddy, I asked you to do something. You wanted to help me, and this is part of helping."

"But…my dad always…" Justin's lower lip pushed out and Kip could see the sparkle of tears in his eyes and his heart melted.

"Oh, buddy," he whispered, pulling Justin in his arms. He gave him a tight squeeze, his own heart contracting in sorrow. It had been only six months since they stood together at Scott's grave. In the busyness of life, he sometimes forgot that. He held Justin a moment longer and as he stood, he caught Nicole looking at them both, her lips pressed together, her fingers resting on her chin.

She understood, he thought, and he wondered if she was remembering her own sister.

Their gaze held and for a moment they shared a sorrow.

The rumbling of the tool chest broke the moment. "I got it. I got it." Tristan called out.

Kip gave Justin another quick hug, patted him on the head and turned back to the tractor with a sigh.

"What do you have to do?" Nicole asked.

"It's a basic fix," Kip said as he pushed a piece of cardboard under the tractor. "Replace a leaky fuel line, but whoever designed this tractor has obviously never worked on one." Kip bent over, squinting at the nuts holding the old line. Then he grabbed the tools he needed, lay on the cardboard and pulled himself under the tractor.

"Justin, why don't you get those rags for your Uncle Kip," he heard Nicole say. "Tristan, maybe you can clean up those bits of wood lying in the corner."

A born organizer, he thought, straining as he tried to pull off a bolt. He was still trying to wrap his head around the woman whom he'd seen in the office this morning—the all-business woman in her stark suit—and the woman wearing blue jeans and a flannel shirt, standing in his shop.

He pushed the picture aside, focussing on the job at hand.

"Tristan, does your Uncle Kip have a broom?" he heard her asking, and a couple of minutes later he heard the swishing of the broom over the concrete floor accompanied by her quiet voice giving directions to the boys to move things out of the way.

He felt a squirm of embarrassment as he worked another nut free, imagining the shop through her eyes. He knew it was a mess. He liked his shop organized and neat but hadn't had the time to tidy it up.

Finally he got the line free, and as he pulled himself out from under the tractor he found the box of rags.

His second surprise was the clean floor and

the boxes of oil and grease stacked neatly in one corner by the compressor. The shop vac sat beside it, the hose attached again and the cord wrapped neatly around the top.

"So when will you need my socket and wrench?" Nicole asked, poking her head around the front of the tractor.

Kip released a short laugh. "Right now."

"So you were serious about that?" she asked, arching a perfectly plucked brow.

"I was joking about you bringing them, but I wasn't joking about needing them." He hadn't been able to find the wrench and socket ever since the boys "helped" him the last time. In his rush to get back to the ranch after seeing Ron, he had forgotten to pick up the tools at the hardware store.

He blew out a sigh of displeasure thinking of yet another trip to town.

"Then I'll go get them," she said.

He frowned. "You have them here?"

"In my car. Shall I get them?" She gave him a wry look.

"If you've got them here, that would be great," he said, completely serious this time.

"Can we come?" Justin and Tristan chimed in.

"Ms. Williams can go by herself," Kip said.

"I'm just going to the car."

"The boys stay here."

Nicole held his gaze a beat, as if reading more into his comment than he meant. Which was fine by him.

"Okay. I'll be back."

Kip watched her go, her blond hair catching the sun, her hands strung up in the pockets of her snug blue jeans.

He didn't need this right now. He looked down at the boys who were watching her go, looking a bit starstruck. Not that he blamed them. She was beautiful, she was attentive.

Only they didn't know was that she was big, big trouble.

Nicole didn't have to look over her shoulder to know Kip was watching her. She felt his eyes drilling into the back of her neck and wished he hadn't insisted on her visiting the boys at the ranch. It was as if she was under constant scrutiny.

When she got to the car she shot a quick look over her shoulder, but she was out of sight of the shed. She pulled out the bag of tools and grabbed her cell phone at the same time.

"Pretty sweet cell phone."

Nicole jumped, then spun around in time to see Isabelle sauntering down the stairs with all the confidence of a sixteen-year-old girl.

"You got any fun games on it?" she asked.

"I don't play games on my phone."

Isabelle slanted her head to one side, her eyes narrowed. "No, but you play games with us. Pretending to be a housekeeper. You know how much trouble I got into because of you?"

"You seemed glad to leave me alone with your mother and all the work," Nicole countered.

"I don't think I like you," Isabelle said, crossing her thin arms over her chest.

"I don't think that matters." Nicole was sure she wasn't well liked by the rest of the Cosgrove family either. She wasn't here to win a popularity contest. She was here to get her father's grandchildren back to him. Her atonement.

"My brother won't let you take Justin and Tristan away from here, you know. He'll fight you."

"I know he will," she answered, checking her voice mail while she spoke. Five new messages. She hit the Answer button as she walked back to the shed, taking the bag of tools with her.

Isabelle followed a few steps behind her.

"Don't you have work to do?" Nicole asked, feeling like was being spied on.

"My mom is sleeping and I don't want to wake her up."

Nicole gave her a vague nod as she skipped through the messages from her assistant, Heather. She could deal with those when she got back to the motel, but the one from the lawyer...

"No news to report yet." Her family's lawyer's

voice was brisk and businesslike, and he didn't waste any words or time. "Still working on the legalities of the will. Should have more information in a couple of days."

Isabelle took a quick step to get ahead of Nicole. "You can't do this to my mother, you know," she said, her voice intense. "She'll die if you take the twins. Those are Scott's boys and he's gone." This was followed by a dramatic sniff.

Nicole caught a flash of her own intensity in the young girl's eyes. Her own reasons for reuniting the boys with her father.

Her step faltered, but for only a moment. "I'm sorry, Isabelle, but I'm not talking to you about this."

She walked past Isabelle toward the garage, shoving her phone into her pocket. As she came near she saw Kip watching her, wiping his hands on a rag. Had he been looking at her the entire time?

"What did you say to my sister?" he asked, pointing his chin toward Isabelle.

Nicole shot a quick glance over her shoulder. Isabelle stood in the middle of the yard, her arms wrapped around her middle, staring at Nicole, her expression tight with anger.

"I told her I wasn't talking to her about the situation." She handed him the tools. "Where are the boys?"

Kip angled his head to the back of the shop and without a word to him, Nicole walked toward them.

But even as she did, her stomach twisted with old, familiar emotions. Again she was on the outside of a family looking in. Sure, she hadn't expected to be accepted and greeted with warmth, but she hadn't counted on how much their antagonism would bother her. Especially when, for a few hours, she had been welcomed by them.

"Auntie Nicole, there you are."

Nicole smiled and looked around. "I can't find you Justin," she called out, warmth flooding her heart at the sound of his voice.

Then a pair of arms flung themselves around her waist and she looked down onto the blond head of a little boy.

As she hugged him back, she felt her own heart crack open just a little wider. She could not let the feelings of the Cosgrove family stand in the way of what she had to do.

Her father's needs came before theirs.

Chapter Six

Nicole pushed the accelerator further down as her car climbed the hill. She had Vivaldi on the stereo, the windows open and her car headed in the direction of the ranch and Tricia's boys.

The highway made a curve, then topped a rise, and Nicole's breath left her. The valley spread out below her, a vast expanse of space yawning for miles, then undulating toward green hills and giving way to imperious mountains, their peaks capped with snow, blinding white against a blue, blue sky.

In spite of her hurry to get to the ranch, she slowed down, taking it all in. The space, the emptiness.

The freedom. She felt the faintest hitch in her soul.

She was a city girl, but somehow this country called to her. Yesterday she'd almost got lost on her way to the ranch because she kept looking around, taking in the view.

She took in a deep breath and let the space and quiet ease into her soul.

Yesterday, after seeing the boys, she'd come back to a raft of emails all dealing with the foundation banquet she and her assistant had been planning. Nicole first sent a quick update to her father, then waded into the work, dealing with whatever came out of them until two. This morning she'd gotten up early and finished up. Then, still tired, she'd grabbed a nap, only she forgot to set her alarm. Now she was an hour and a half late for her meeting with the boys.

The ringing of her cell phone made her jump. She blew out a frustrated sigh, glanced at the caller ID and forced a smile.

"What did the lawyer say?" her father asked.

Sam Williams may have been ill, but he hadn't lost his capacity of getting straight to the point.

"The usual lawyer stuff," Nicole said tucking a strand of hair behind her ear that the wind coming into the car had pulled free from her ponytail. "Things are going to take time. He needs to verify Tricia's will. Nothing definite."

"How are the boys?"

"I wish you could see them. They're so cute." A picture of them pushing the oversize broom in their uncle's shop yesterday made her smile. "They're such little cowboys."

Her father didn't say anything to that and Nicole guessed it was the wrong response.

"I'll try to call from the ranch today," Nicole said. "See if you can talk to them."

"The new school year starts in three months," her father said as Nicole turned onto the road leading to the ranch. "I'm looking into schools for them."

As Sam spoke, Nicole's thoughts slipped back to Kip's comment about putting the boys on the bus and his obvious regret. At least he wouldn't have to deal with that come September.

"I'm getting to a bad area and I'll be losing reception. I'll try to call you from the ranch."

"If I was feeling better I'd be there…"

The rest of her father's words were cut off when Nicole's car dropped into the valley.

As Nicole turned onto the ranch's driveway, she felt another clutch of frustration at Kip Cosgrove's insistence that she visit the boys only at the ranch.

How was she supposed to get to know her nephews in two and a half hours under his watchful eye? But as she came around the corner, her frustration gave way to anticipation at the thought of seeing the boys again.

As Nicole parked her car beside Kip's huge

pickup she jumped out of the car, looked around, but didn't see anyone. She walked to the house and knocked on the door.

Nothing.

Where was everybody? She lifted her hand to knock again when she saw a note on the door addressed to her.

"In the field. Moving bales. Mom sleeping." The words were hastily scribbled on a small piece of paper and stuck to the door with a piece of masking tape.

Nicole blew out a sigh. Which field? How was she supposed to find them? She could almost hear the clock ticking down the precious seconds on her visit.

She paused, listening, then heard the sound of a tractor. Thankfully, it sounded like it was coming closer.

She jogged across the yard, past the chuck wagons. As she raced around a corner of the barn, a tractor lurched into view pulling a wagon loaded up with hay. Smoke billowed from the stack and the engine roared, a deafening sound in the once-stillness.

The sun reflected off the glass of the closed-in cab of the tractor, but as it came closer, Nicole saw Kip driving and Justin and Tristan standing behind the seat.

With a squeal of brakes the tractor came to

a halt beside her and Kip opened the side door. "You're late," he yelled over the noise of the tractor's engine.

Like she needed him to tell her that.

"Yes. Sorry." What else could she say?

Justin leaned over Kip's shoulder and waved at her. "Hey, Ms. Williams," he shouted.

Ms. Williams? What happened to Auntie Nicole?

Nicole just smiled and waved, quite sure Kip had something to do with the change.

She walked to the tractor, raising her arms to take the boys out. "Hey, Tristan. You boys helping Mr. Cosgrove?" Two could play that game.

Tristan gave her a puzzled look. Nicole could tell that Kip understood exactly what she was doing.

"We just have to unload these bales." Kip closed the door before she came any closer and before the boys could get out. He put the tractor in gear and drove away.

She was left to trail behind the swaying wagon, fuming as bits of hay swirled around her face. With each step her anger at his pettiness grew. He was depriving her of valuable time with her own nephews so he could prove a point.

She easily kept up with the tractor and followed it to where she assumed he was going to pile up these bales. But neither he nor the boys got out of the tractor. Somehow he unhitched the wagon from inside, turned the tractor around and started to unload the bales. One at a time.

She was reduced to watching as the clock ticked away precious minutes of her visiting time.

Kip reminded her of her biological father and how he used to make her wait in the motel room while he busied himself with who knew what in his truck while her aunt fumed. Older, buried emotions slipped to the fore. As she had done the first few years at Sam and Norah's, she fought them down. She was here and she had a job to do for her father. That was all she had to focus on.

She waited until the last bale was unloaded and then she marched over to the tractor before Kip could decide he had to go for another load and leave her behind.

But just as she reached the tractor, Kip shut it off and the door opened.

"You finally came," Tristan called out.

The "finally" added to her burden of guilt, and she gave them a quick smile. "Yes, I'm sorry I was late," she said as Kip lifted Tristan up and over the seat.

"Got busy with work?" he asked as she reached up to take Tristan from him.

"Forgot to set my alarm," was her terse reply as she set Tristan down on the ground. He didn't need to know that to some degree he was right and she was surprised that he had guessed, at least partially, why she was late.

He made a show of looking at his watch. "You city people keep crazy hours."

"I was working late and grabbed a nap," she said trying not to rise to his goading.

"So you were working."

"I have to do something while I'm waiting around for my appointed visiting times," she snapped. "Justin, honey, tell Mr. Cosgrove that he's working on a Saturday too and we're wasting time here."

Justin frowned, then laughed. "He is Uncle Kip," the little boy said with a grin.

"He is many things," Nicole returned, her gaze still on Kip.

His eyes narrowed as if he caught the inference but wasn't sure what to do with it. Instead of saying anything, he handed Justin down to her.

"I'm taking the boys to see the puppies. Is that okay?" she asked.

"Just stay away from the horses. I'm going back for another load of hay," he said, his voice brusque. "Make sure you keep the boys away from the tractor too when I come back."

Before she could think of a suitable reply, he had closed the door and started up the tractor again.

She bit her anger back, took a breath to calm herself, then looked down at the boys. No sense in letting them know how angry she was with their uncle.

"Let's go," the boys said, dragging her by the hand toward the barn.

"We'll first go see your grandmother and then we'll go see the puppies," Nicole said.

They ran across the yard ahead of her, laughing and screaming like two young colts.

Nicole smiled at the picture of utter freedom.

When Nicole and the boys got to the house, Mary was watching television. She brightened when the boys came into the living room.

"Hey, there, my boys. Do you want to watch a movie with me?" she asked.

Nicole was about to protest.

"Can we watch *Robin Hood?*" Justin asked before she could speak.

"I'll go get it," Tristan said.

Nicole stifled a beat of disappointment. She'd hoped to spend her time with the boys alone, just the three of them. She had looked forward to being outside with them, walking around the ranch, not sitting inside a stuffy house watching television.

But Mary was their grandmother and she was simply the outsider, so she said nothing.

The boys popped the movie in and settled on the couch to watch. Nicole sat with them for a bit but got fidgety. She'd never enjoyed watching television like her sister did. She had preferred reading and doing crafts.

"Do you mind if I tidy up?" she said to Mary.

"You don't have to do our work," Mary protested, pushing herself up as if to get up out of her wheelchair.

"I don't mind. I'm not much of a television person, and I don't mind, really. You sit with the boys and I'll wander around here."

Though she had grown up with a housekeeper, years of living in foster homes had given Nicole a measure of independence, and she had always kept her own room neat and later on, she did her own laundry.

So Nicole tidied and cleaned, washed dishes and did another load of laundry while the boys sat mindlessly in front of the television.

What a shame, she thought, wishing she had enough authority to turn off the television and make them come outside.

Finally, the movie was over and Nicole came into the living room. "I think we should go outside now."

"I'll have a nap," Mary said. She smiled at the boys. "Now don't go and tell your Uncle Kip." She winked at them and they giggled. Then she glanced at Nicole. "Kip doesn't let them watch television during the day."

If she'd known that, Nicole thought, she wouldn't

have let them. But she didn't know the politics and the hierarchy of this particular household, though she was learning.

She turned to the boys. "Now you'll have to show me where those puppies are," she said. They each took one of her hands and as she looked down at their upraised faces a wave of love washed over her.

It surprised her and, if she were honest, frightened her. Each time she saw them it was as if one more hook was attached to her heart. The pain of letting go could be too much.

But that wouldn't happen, she reminded herself, holding even more tightly to their hands. The boys were Tricia's and were never Scott's no matter what Kip might believe. She and her father had the law on their side.

They stepped outside and Nicole inhaled the fresh, pure air. It was so wonderful to be outdoors.

"I want to see the horses," Justin said as they stepped off the porch.

"Your uncle said it wasn't allowed." And there was no way she was running afoul of Kip while on his ranch.

"If we're real careful, it will be okay."

"Not on your life," Nicole said firmly.

Justin sighed. "That's what Uncle Kip always says too."

One more thing we have in common, Nicole thought with a sense of irony.

"So where are these puppies?" she asked.

"They're in the barn."

As they walked, the boys, mostly Justin, brought her up to date on what Uncle Kip had done this morning—first he cut himself shaving, then he listened to the market report and made breakfast, then he tried to get Gramma to do her exercises.

What their grandmother had done—sat and watched television.

What Isabelle had done—slept in and got into trouble with Uncle Kip.

"Isabelle is fun. Uncle Kip says she has to grow up, but she's pretty big already."

Nicole suspected that Uncle Kip had his hands full with his sister. Isabelle needed a firm hand and guidance. Something, she suspected, Kip was at a loss to enforce.

Justin pulled open the large, heavy barn door then he stopped and held his finger to his lips. "I better go in first because we don't want to scare the mommy dog," he whispered. "I'll call you when you can come in."

He walked slowly into the barn and Tristan seemed content to stay behind with Nicole.

The only sound breaking the stillness was the shuffle of Justin's feet on the barn floor and the song of a few birds that Nicole couldn't identify. She listened, and the quiet pressed down on her ears.

The silence spread out everywhere, huge and overwhelming. For the briefest moment, icy fingers of panic gripped her heart. They were far away from the nearest road, the nearest town.

All alone.

Then she looked down at Tristan, smiling shyly up at her. She watched Justin creeping into the dusty barn. They were completely relaxed here, at home and at peace.

"And a little child shall lead them."

The familiar passage drifted into her mind and she puzzled it over, wondering where it had come from.

Then she remembered. It was from the Bible. Her mother used to read the Bible to her and Tricia.

"You hold my hand almost as tight as Uncle Kip does when we're in Calgary," Tristan whispered.

Nicole started. "I'm sorry," she said, loosening her grip. "I didn't mean to hurt you."

He smiled up at her. "That's okay. Uncle Kip always says he holds tight because he never wants to let us go. That makes me feel good."

Nicole's heart faltered at his words. Of course the boys would be attached to Kip Cosgrove and he to them. This was the only life the boys had known.

But they weren't Cosgroves, she reminded herself. They were Williamses, in spite of what Kip may claim.

Yet as she followed Justin into the dusky coolness of the barn, she felt her own misgivings come to the fore. Her own memories of being moved from home to home.

But she never returned to her biological home, like these boys were going to. She could never go back to where the people she lived with were related to her by blood, but these boys could. She would give them the true family she'd never had and in doing so, maybe, just maybe—

Her thoughts were cut off by the ringing of her phone.

It was her father.

"Hey," she whispered, following Tristan into the dusty pen. The floor was strewn with straw and Justin was crouched in the corner, his behind stuck in the air as he reached under a pile of lumber.

"Can you talk?"

"Yes. I'm with the boys."

"I want to talk to them. Now."

Nicole hesitated. This was the first time she'd been alone with the boys since she'd met them. She hadn't had an opportunity to let them know that not only did they have another aunt, they also had a grandfather. She highly doubted Kip Cosgrove let them know either.

"I haven't explained everything to them yet—"

"You're telling me they don't know about me?"

Her father's gruff voice created a storm of guilt in Nicole. "I haven't found the right time to tell them," she whispered.

Justin wriggled backwards then turned around with a triumphant grin. He held up a squirming, mewling puppy. The little creature was a bundle of brown and black fur with a shiny button nose.

"I got one," he squealed. Nicole knelt down, still holding the phone as Justin brought the puppy over to her. "You want to hold it?" he asked.

"That's one of them, isn't it?" her father asked. He broke into a fit of coughing, a sure sign to Nicole that he was upset. "I need to talk to them. Please, let me talk to them."

It was the please that was her undoing. She couldn't remember her father saying those words more than a dozen times in her life.

"Just give me a few seconds," she whispered to her father. "I need to explain a few things." She smiled at Justin and held out her hand. "Yes, I'd love to hold it," she said. "Why don't you hold my phone for me and I'll take the puppy?"

Justin managed to release his grip on the puppy and take the phone. Nicole gathered the warm, silky bundle in her arms, her heart melting at the sight of its chocolate-brown eyes staring soulfully up at her. She crouched down in the straw covering the floor of the pen, preferring not to think what might be living in it.

"He likes you," Tristan said as she settled down.

"Who are you talking to?" Justin asked, looking at her phone.

"Why don't you come and sit by me," she said, keeping her voice low and quiet. "I have something to tell you."

Curious, Justin knelt down in front of her, still holding the phone, Tristan beside her. She stroked the puppy and looked from one pair of trusting eyes to the other. "You know that you had a mommy, right?"

"We don't know where our mommy is," Justin said. "She ranned away."

Nicole pressed back an angry reply. Their lack of knowledge wasn't their fault. "Your mommy didn't run away," she said. "Your mommy loved you both very much, and your mommy had a father who loved her very much too. That father is your grandmother."

"Our grandpa is dead," Justin said. "Uncle Kip told us."

"Now you know that you have another grandfather," Nicole said. "And he's alive and he lives in Toronto."

"You mean like Paul and Liam and Kirsten and Leah and Emily and Jenna from Auntie Doreen? They have a grandpa," Tristan squealed. "Uncle Ron's daddy."

"That's right."

"Where is our other grandfather?" Justin asked.

"I was talking to him on the phone you're holding," Nicole said, tilting her head toward the phone Justin clutched. "You can talk to him if you want."

Justin frowned. "Uncle Kip lets me pretend to talk on his phone," he said.

"You don't have to pretend," Nicole said gently. "Now I'll hit a button and put it on speakerphone so we can all hear all of us talk." She tapped her phone, then held it out. "Justin, say hello to your grandfather."

Justin lifted his shoulders, suddenly self-conscious. "Are you my grandpa? This is Justin."

"Yes, I am. How are you?"

Justin frowned, then said, "I'm fine. How are you?"

She heard a faint cough, then her father replied that he was fine.

Nicole let Justin chatter on about the puppies

and hauling hay. Her father made a few responses, but he didn't have to say much around Justin.

"Father, this is Tristan. He wants to say hi," Nicole said, taking the phone away from Justin.

Tristan was more reserved, but soon he was giving out information as freely as his brother.

The phone distorted her father's voice but it wasn't hard to hear the joy in it. Joy she hadn't heard in her father's voice since Tricia left home.

"Hey there, did you guys find the puppies?"

Nicole jumped, startling the puppy, then she craned her neck backwards to see Kip standing in the doorway.

What was he doing? Checking up on her?

"What are you doing with Ms. Williams's phone?" Kip asked, frowning at Tristan.

Tristan looked up, his smile dropping away as soon as he saw his Uncle Kip.

"We're talking to our grandpa," Justin announced. "He said we are going to stay with him. In Toronto. Can we go, Uncle Kip? Can we?"

Nicole's heart dropped when she saw the thunderous expression cross Kip's face.

"I think you should give the phone back to Ms. Williams, then go back to the house."

"I want to talk to my other grandfather some more," Justin whined.

"Tristan, please give the phone back to Ms. Williams and go with Justin to the house."

Nicole glanced at the little boy who was obviously listening to something her father was saying. Tristan looked from Kip to Nicole, confusion on his features.

"Don't go," she heard her father say. "Don't listen to him."

She had to put poor Tristan out of his misery.

"I'll take the phone, sweetie," she said holding her hand out.

"No. Nicole. I need to talk to them."

"Sorry, Father," she said quietly. She turned the phone off speaker, then walked away from Kip. "The boys have to go."

"Those boys shouldn't be there," her father said. "They should be here with me."

"I know, but not everything is settled yet."

Her father started coughing again, then got his breath. "I'm phoning that lawyer first thing Monday morning. We shouldn't have to wait for these DNA tests. We know Tricia was their mother."

Nicole glanced over her shoulder at Kip standing in the doorway of the barn watching the boys walk to the house. Obviously he was sticking around to talk to her. "We have to move slowly on this," she said to her father.

"Those boys have to come back to their home,"

he said quietly. "You of all people know why Tricia's boys need to come back."

As always, his words held a subtext of obligation that was never spoken directly but always hinted at. "Of course I do," she replied. "I have to go." As she said goodbye, she felt a moment of sympathy for her father, all alone back home.

She couldn't help comparing his lonely situation to Mary Cosgrove's. Mary had one daughter with six grandchildren and she had another daughter and son and two more grandchildren under her roof.

The boys weren't Cosgroves. It was as if she had to drum that information into her mind. If she didn't, then she would start to feel sorry for Mary.

And for Kip.

She pocketed her phone and turned to face Kip.

"Why did you do that?" he demanded.

Any sympathy she might have felt for the man was brushed away in the icy blast of his question.

"If you're thinking I deliberately brought the boys out here so they could talk to my father on the phone, you're mistaken. He just happened to call while I was out here."

"And you just happened to let the boys talk to him."

"May I remind you that he's their grandfather?"

"That hasn't been proven beyond a doubt."

"You were willing to let me visit them based on
this doubt."

Kip's eyes narrowed and she knew she had gone
too far. "Only because my lawyer told me I should.
No other reason."

Nicole knew Kip had not let her willingly onto
the farm. She was here on suffrage only. "Regardless of how you see the situation, the man I just
spoke to is Tricia's father—"

"And he was never part of the agreement." Kip
took a step closer and it was all Nicole could do
to keep her cool. "You're not to let the boys talk to
your father again without talking to me about it,"
he warned, his voice lowering to a growl. "Those
poor kids lost their father six months ago, and they
don't need to have any more confusion in their
lives."

Nicole struggled to hold his steely gaze. "Find-
ing out that they have a maternal grandfather can
hardly be confusing to any child. In fact, many
people would see it as a blessing."

That last comment came out before she could
stop it, as did the tiny hitch in her voice. She hoped
he would put it down to her anger rather than the
fact that she had found herself jealous of these
boys. Jealous of Kip.

He had family that had no strings attached. A mother who doted on him and a sister who, in spite of her rebellious ways, still cared for him. He didn't have to try to earn his mother's love, try to atone for what he did.

Kip's mouth settled into a grim line and she felt as if she scored the tiniest point.

"That may be, but at the same time I'm their uncle and guardian and responsible for their well-being. Anything you do with them gets run by me. The boys are my first priority, not you, or your father."

Nicole bit back a retort, realizing that to some degree he was right. Much as it bothered her, she couldn't argue with him.

Kip shoved his hand through his hair and released a heavy sigh. "I've got too much happening right now. I can't give the boys the explanations they will need if you start complicating their lives."

Nicole held his gaze and for a moment in spite of her anger with him, sympathy stirred in her soul. Sympathy and something more profound. Respect, even. Regardless of whatever claim Nicole may have, the reality was that this man was putting as a first priority the welfare of two little boys that weren't his children. Even though his guardianship put them at odds, at the same time she respected what he was doing.

She thought of how easily her biological father seemed to give her up. How happy her aunt had been when Social Services came to take her away for good. In spite of her aunt's antagonism, Nicole had wished that she could stay, but her aunt wanted her gone.

Those boys don't know how good they had it. In fact, Nicole was jealous that they had this strong, tough man on their side. A man who had made sacrifices for his nephews. A man who was willing to fight for them.

What would have happened in her earlier life if she'd had the same kind of advocate? If she'd had someone who was willing to go to the mat for her welfare? What if she'd had someone like Kip on her side?

"I'd like you to leave now," Kip said quietly.

Nicole opened her mouth to protest.

"It's past five," Kip said.

"Of course," was all she said. "I'll be back tomorrow then."

Kip just nodded.

Nicole got up and walked past him, then got into her car. As she drove off, she could see him in her rearview mirror watching her.

He could watch and glower all he wanted. She wasn't letting him intimidate her.

She had rights and she was going to exercise them regardless of what he thought of her.

Chapter Seven

"I'm not doing the dishes again." Isabelle glared at Kip, her hands on her hips. "Sunday is a day of rest. At least that's what I thought the minister said."

As Kip tried to match her glare for glare he also tried not to feel guilty about all the work he hoped to get done today.

"I'm not your slave," she muttered.

He ignored that. "Just make sure the dishes get done," he growled. Then he turned to his mother. "And you make sure she does it and don't you even think about doing it yourself."

Mary gave him a quick nod, which didn't give Kip much confidence.

Didn't any of the women in his life listen to him? He spun around just as he heard a knock on the door.

What was Nicole doing here already?

"Tristan. Justin," he called out. "Finish up. Ms. Williams is here." He sent the boys upstairs to change out of their Sunday clothes about an hour ago and they still weren't down.

"It's not fair, you know," Isabelle whined, leaning back against the counter.

Nicole stepped into the kitchen. "Um…I think you have a problem," she said. "There are some cows roaming around the yard," she continued. "I'm guessing they're not supposed to be there."

"What?" Kip frowned, then as her words registered, he pushed past her and stepped outside, then groaned in disbelief.

Over two dozen cows and calves were milling about out of the fence.

There went the afternoon, Kip thought, his heart dropping into his gut. His mind flipped through all the scenarios why the animals would be loose. Open gate. Broken fence.

Not that it mattered. For now he had to get them away from the hay bales, and even more important, away from the granary filled with oats.

"What can I do?" Nicole asked.

Was she kidding? Kip spared her a quick glance then strode down the steps. "Just stay out of the way."

Not that he had a master plan that she could help him implement. He was pretty much winging it.

As he got closer to the moving herd he slowed

his steps, planning, thinking. The gate to the pasture wasn't open, so that left one thing. Broken fences.

He shifted his hat back on his head as he glanced around the yard, trying to figure out what to do with the herd. Where to put them.

They started moving and he hurried his steps, trying to get ahead of them without spooking them.

Of course, one cow let out a bawl, spun around and they all decided to change their focus and head down the driveway.

"No, you stupid creatures," he yelled, moving even more quickly.

Please, Lord, don't let them head down the driveway. Because once they did, they would be on the run and it would take hours and hours to get them back again.

He changed direction and ran, knowing he didn't stand a chance of getting them turned around. Not on foot and not without his horse, but he had to try.

Sweat poured down his back, anger clenched his gut and then, suddenly he heard, "Hey. Get back there."

He looked up and there were Nicole and Isabelle standing by the driveway waving dishtowels. Were they kidding? Dishtowels against two dozen 1,200-pound cows on the loose?

Miraculously the cows stopped, dust slowly settling around them. Kip caught his breath, trying to assess. Then a calf broke free from the herd but again, to his surprise Nicole got the animal turned around.

"Let's get them into the corrals," he called out. "Isabelle, can you get to the gate?"

"No," she said, glaring at him.

"This is not the time, missy," he called back.

Thankfully, Nicole moved over to the fence and climbed over it, leaving Isabelle standing guard. Even from here Kip could see the fear on Nicole's face, but surprisingly she kept moving.

She opened the gate to the pasture, then came back over the fence, staying clear of the cows.

"Start moving slowly toward them," Kip called out. "Don't get right in front of them. Work at them from the side."

Nicole nodded and started walking at an angle toward the herd. It was probably a good thing she was afraid. She moved slowly and took her time.

"Stop there, Nicole," Kip yelled.

Kip moved toward the herd just enough to get them going. Then, thankfully, the cows in the lead turned around. The ones behind them followed their example, and soon the herd was turned around and walking back to the pasture.

Please, please, he prayed as he moved slowly behind them, keeping them moving. If they turned around now, they would scatter and it could easily take all day to get them herded up again.

The cows at the head of the herd sped up the pace. It was going to be all right, Kip thought.

Suddenly one of the cows in the middle turned her head and decided to make a break for it.

Right toward Nicole.

She stood, frozen, as another cow followed the one trying to get away. This was it. They were hooped.

Then Nicole waved her arms and yelled and to Kip's surprise the cow stopped and rejoined the herd now heading into the corral.

"Isabelle, get over the fence and make sure they don't get into the pasture," Kip called out.

"Are you kidding?" Isabelle said. "I'm going back to the house."

"Oh, stop being such a selfish stinker and just do what your brother said," Nicole shouted back at her.

Kip didn't know who was more surprised at Nicole's outburst, him or his sister.

At any rate, Isabelle scrambled over the fence and headed off the cows that were eyeing the wide-open spaces of the pasture. Then, thankfully, the cows were all in the corral and Kip closed the metal gate, locking them in.

"So is that all of them?" Nicole's voice sounded a bit shaky as she joined them.

"Those were only a small part of the whole herd. Now I have to saddle up and find out where they got out and then make sure that the rest of the cows are where they're supposed to be." He dragged his hand over his face, thinking.

"I know this might sound dumb, but is there anything I can do?"

Kip glanced down at her. Some wisps of hair had pulled loose from her ponytail and were curling around her face. Her cheeks were flushed and she had a smear of dust on her forehead. She looked a bit scared yet, but she also looked kinda cute.

"Not really, but thanks for all your help. I couldn't have done it without you."

"And Isabelle," Nicole said wryly.

"Thanks for bawling her out. Nice to know I'm not the only one doing it."

Nicole laughed at that. "I'm real good at bawling out little sisters. I did it all the time with Tricia." She stopped there as an expression of deep sorrow slid over her face.

Kip wondered what she meant by her comment. What created that look of desolate sadness?

"Are you okay?" he asked.

Puzzlement replaced the sadness. "Why do you ask?"

He frowned. "You looked so sad. I'm thinking you're remembering your sister. I guess I know what it feels like."

She looked up at him then. Their gazes locked and held as awareness arced between them.

Without thinking of the implications he laid his hand on her shoulder, as if to cement the connection.

She looked away, but didn't move.

A yearning slipped through him. A yearning for things to be different between them. Involuntarily, his hand tightened.

"Nicole—"

"Uncle Kip, Uncle Kip. Isabelle said the cows got out…Did you get them in?…Can we help… Do you have to ride the horses?"

The boys burst into the moment with a barrage of questions and Nicole stepped away. As Kip lowered his hand, he experienced a surprising sense of loss. Then he gave his head a shake.

What was he thinking? This woman was simply another problem in his complicated life.

Kip dragged his attention back to his nephews. "Yeah. I'll be saddling up and heading out."

"Can we ride with you?" Justin asked.

Kip shot him a warning glance. The little guy knew better.

"Why don't we go and check out the puppies," Nicole said, taking the boys by their hands. "Have they gotten any bigger?"

"Silly, you just saw them yesterday," Justin said.

"I know, but puppies grow very fast and change

quickly," she replied. "I would hate to think that we missed out on something fun that they didn't do yesterday."

Kip was sure her comment was off the cuff, but it reminded him of all the changes he'd experienced with the boys. All the changes she and her father had missed.

You can't start going there, he reminded himself. You have a lawyer working to make sure the boys stay here. She has a lawyer to make sure the boys go with her.

Very straightforward. Cut-and-dried.

Yet just before she left she shot a glance over her shoulder, her hair brushing her cheek. Then she gave him a quick smile and things got confusing again. Thankfully he was going out on his horse. Things always got clearer for him when he was in the saddle.

He headed out to the tack shed, and as he opened the door the scent of leather and neat's foot oil washed over him. He halted as recollections of his brother surfaced from the corner of his mind where he thought he'd buried them.

He and Scott racing each other through pastures. He and Scott training the horses, racing the chucks, dust roiling out behind them, the horses' hooves pounding, the adrenaline flowing.

He grabbed the door frame, steadying himself against the onslaught of memories.

Dear Lord, help me get through this, he prayed, bowing his head as pain mingled with the memories. He missed his brother. He missed their time together, but mixed with the sorrow was the sad reality that he missed the freedom he'd had before his brother died.

The insidious thought crept into his mind. How much easier and freer his life would be if he didn't have the boys. How much simpler. The obligations of their future hung on his shoulders as well. Providing for them, taking care of their future.

Kip reached for his saddle and jerked it off the stand, shaking his head as if dislodging the thought. They were his brother's boys, his mother's grandchildren. They were not a burden.

A few minutes later he had saddled his horse, Duke, and was riding out, leaving the ranch house and all the tangle of family obligations behind for a while.

Again he sent up a prayer for clarity of thought, and as he rode, as the sun warmed his back and the wind cooled his face, peace settled into his soul.

This was how he used to spend his Sundays, just riding around or working with the horses.

Now work piled on top of work, and quiet time for himself was as rare as a date, something else he hadn't had in months. He let his thoughts dwell for a moment on his horses. He should work with them. For their sake, if not his.

But when?

He looked around him, at the hills surrounding the ranch. A group of cows lay on one hill, beyond them another bunch. Thankfully, they hadn't decided to follow the wayward cows that had managed to get out.

Though he still had the same amount of work as he'd had before, riding out on his horse loosened the tension gripping his neck. Checking fences was one of his favorite jobs. Just him and his horse and the quiet. Oh, how he missed the quiet.

The irony was, he wouldn't have been able to do this if it wasn't for Nicole being with the boys and watching over his mother. Much as he hated to admit it, since she'd started visiting, some of his responsibilities had eased off his shoulders.

At the same time, Nicole presented a whole nest of problems that complicated his life. He thought again of that moment they'd shared a moment ago.

He wished he could shake it off. Wished he could get her out of his mind.

"I'm just a lonely old cowboy," he said to Duke as he dismounted and stapled up another loose wire. "I've got responsibilities out the wazoo, and once this thing is settled with the boys, my life can go back to normal crazy instead of super crazy."

Duke whickered, tossing his head as if sympathizing with him.

Kip checked the wire and got on the horse again. Duke started walking, the sound of his muffled footfalls creating a soothing rhythm.

Except he couldn't get rid of the nagging feeling that things would not be settled with the boys. Not without a fight.

"C'mon, Auntie Nicole. Hurry up." Tristan's disembodied voice came from somewhere ahead of her on the narrow trail through the trees.

Nicole slowed down and stepped over an exposed rock on the trail, then pushed past a clump of spruce trees.

"Slow down," she puffed, pushing aside a spruce branch that threatened to blind her. "I can't go as fast as you." Not for the first time was she thankful she had bought some running shoes. Keeping up with the boys would have been impossible in the leather boots that she, at one time, had considered casual wear.

When she'd arrived this afternoon the boys had grabbed her and insisted she come and see something important. They wouldn't tell her what, only that she had to come right now.

She caught a glimpse of Tristan's striped T-shirt as she clambered over a fallen tree, then clambered over another one.

"Are you coming?" she heard Justin call out.

"Yes, I'm coming." She drew in a ragged breath,

then, finally, she came to a small clearing. She ducked to get under a tree and as she straightened, looked around.

She couldn't see the boys. "Where are you guys?"

She heard giggling above her and looked up.

Two grinning faces stared down at her from a platform anchored between two aspen trees.

"What is this?" she asked, smiling back at the boys.

"It's Uncle Kip and our dad's Robin Hood tree house." They stood up and then disappeared again, only to reappear higher up on another platform. "Come up and see."

"Is it safe?" she asked. If Kip and his brother had been the architects of this tree house, then it had be at least twenty years old.

"Yup," was all they said.

Nicole walked around and found a ladder constructed of branches leaning up against the tree. She tested it and then slowly climbed up. When she got to the platform, she saw Justin, about six trees over, swinging from a rope.

"Justin, would you stop that," she called out.

"It's okay, Auntie Nicole," Tristan assured her. "Uncle Kip said we could play here. He helped fix it up so we could."

Nicole stepped onto the platform and, holding onto an overhanging tree branch for support, looked around.

She saw ropes and bridges and catwalks and more platforms strung between trees edging the clearing. A veritable hideout and a boy's dream come true. "You said your Uncle Kip made this?"

"Yup, he did," Justin called back, still swinging from the rope. "His dad helped him and our dad."

Nicole leaned against the tree behind her and tried to imagine Kip as a young boy working on this tree fort with his father and his brother.

A smile played over her lips as she watched the boys clambering from one structure to another like monkeys. Again she envied them their freedom. How many young boys wouldn't love to have their life?

"Come on back now," she said, glancing at her watch. It was getting close to the end of her visit. Yesterday she had stayed a bit longer and Isabelle had made a snarky comment, which she had ignored.

At the same time, she didn't want to cause any problems. Especially not when the legal status of the boys seemed to be, at least in Kip's eyes, in limbo.

"Can't we play a little longer?" Justin called out.

"No. We have to get back." Nicole tried to sound

firm, but failed. She wasn't in any rush to go back either. The smell of the woods, the sun filtering through the canopy of leaves above and the gentle stillness of the woods eased away the tensions of the day.

She had spent most of her morning on the telephone playing telephone tag with caterers, trying to get a better deal from the venue and sweet-talking various sponsors for the foundation's annual fund-raiser.

More than that, she was having so much fun following the boys around the farm and exploring with them. She couldn't remember the last time she'd simply taken time off and done nothing constructive whatsoever. Even her holidays were usually slotted around conventions or business trips with her father.

She eased out a sigh and slipped down the tree, wrapping her arms around her knees as she watched the boys clamber from tree to tree, yelling and daring each other to go higher, farther, faster.

"Look at me, Auntie Nicole," Justin called out. "I'm flying."

"Me too," Tristan said, determined not to be outdone.

Nicole watched, and applauded and made appropriate noises of admiration.

Reluctantly she glanced at her watch again. Now she really had to go.

"C'mon boys. Let's get back to the house," she said, getting to her feet.

"Just a few more minutes."

"Nope. We have to go. Now." She was already twenty minutes past her visiting time. All she could do was hope Kip was still busy welding and wouldn't notice. She climbed down the ladder to let the boys know she meant business and reluctantly they followed her.

"Can we come here again tomorrow?" Justin asked.

"Of course we can." Nicole looked behind her once more with a smile. Maybe she'd stop in town and pick up some treats. They could have a picnic.

Nicole heard the hum of the welder coming from the shop as they got nearer the house and felt a surge of relief. Kip was still busy.

"What's that smell?" Justin said, wrinkling his nose.

"Smells like—"

"Something's burning," Nicole said. She dropped the boys' hands, took the stairs two at a time and burst into the house.

Mary was leaning on the counter with one hand as she struggled to pull a pan out of the oven with the other.

Smoke billowed out of the oven and the smoke detector started screeching.

"Let me do that," Nicole said, grabbing a tea towel as the boys followed her into the kitchen, hands clapped over their ears and yelling questions.

Ignoring the boys and the piercing shriek of the smoke detector, Nicole rescued a blackened casserole dish from the oven, set it on top of the stove and turned the oven off.

Then she supported Mary and helped her back to her chair.

"Open the back door," she called out to the boys above the ear-piercing shriek as she slid open the window above the sink. "Where's the smoke detector?" she yelled at Mary.

Mary pointed to the hallway off the kitchen and Nicole grabbed a couple of tea towels. She flapped the towels at the detector, the noise piercing through her brain. Justin and Tristan joined her. "We'll help you," they called out, waving their hands at the ceiling.

Nicole laughed at the sight, but kept flapping. Then the smoke detector abruptly quit and peaceful silence fell on the house.

"That was very loud," Tristan said, digging his finger in his ear, as if to dislodge the noise.

"You boys were big helpers," she said, patting them on the head as they walked back to the kitchen.

"Thank you so much," Mary said. "I could smell something boiling over for a while from my bedroom, but I thought Isabelle was watching the casserole."

"I was," Isabelle said, finally making an appearance from upstairs. "I had to make a phone call." Isabelle glanced at Nicole. "What are you doing here?"

"What you should have been doing." Nicole brushed past the sullen girl, and moved to the oven, wincing at the streaked, black goop baked onto the side of the casserole dish. From the condition of the dish and its contents, the phone call had been lengthy.

Nicole found a knife in the sink and pried the lid off the pot, making a face at the burnt mess inside. "There's not much left of this."

"Well, so much for dinner," Mary said with a heavy sigh. "Isabelle, did you forget to turn the oven down after the first ten minutes?"

"I guess."

Nicole glanced around the kitchen. Potato peelings and carrot scrapings filled the sink. The counter was covered with bowls and empty plastic bags and pots. She glanced back at Mary, who was struggling to her feet as if to start making supper all over again. The poor woman looked exhausted.

Nicole tried to imagine herself in the same situation. However, living with her father, they had a housekeeper and a cook who came in three times a week. And she didn't have a son, a teenage daughter and two young boys to cook for.

She made a sudden decision. "Don't worry about supper," she said, shooting a glance at Kip's sister. "Isabelle and I will pull something together."

"What?" Isabelle exclaimed.

"Why don't we go through the refrigerator and see what we can do?" She gave Isabelle a sweet smile, as if challenging her to protest.

Isabelle simply rolled her eyes and sighed.

"Can we help too?" Tristan and Justin asked.

"Of course," Nicole exclaimed. "You guys will be our biggest helpers."

At least this way she could spend the rest of her time with the boys, Nicole thought.

She didn't want to think how Kip would react. He would just have to accept it.

Chapter Eight

What was Nicole still doing here?

Kip glanced at his watch, pushing down a beat of anger. Six-ten. She was supposed to have left over an hour ago.

He forced his frustration back as he toed off his boots on the verandah, then stepped inside the house to speak to Ms. Williams.

The first thing he noticed was the clean counters. Then an unfamiliar but savory smell.

His mother sat in a chair directing Tristan on how to set the knives by the plates on the table, which was covered with a tablecloth. He didn't even know his mother owned a tablecloth. Isabelle was washing dishes and Nicole stood beside her, wearing an apron, her hair tied back, drying a bowl. She handed the bowl to Justin who sat on the counter beside her and he put it in the cupboard.

The kitchen was a rare picture of domestic bliss, with Nicole running point.

He glanced over at Nicole just as she looked back over her shoulder. Her cheeks were flushed, her eyes bright, and she was smiling a genuine smile that gave his heart a lift.

A smile that faded when she saw him.

He shouldn't care, he thought, pushing his reaction to the back of his mind. He had too many things going to be concerned about her reaction to him. On Monday he'd picked up the stuff for the DNA test, gotten everything done just the way the instructions had told him, then ran it all back to town on Tuesday. It was easier than he thought and though he didn't have time to do all the running around, he wanted that whole business out of the way. Now he didn't have to think about it anymore.

"I thought Isabelle was making supper," he grumbled, walking over to the table. He bent over and touched his mother's shoulder lightly. "How are you feeling?"

Mary smiled up at him as well. "Much better. I got up and around a bit. Nicole helped me with my exercises."

"Making yourself indispensable?" Kip asked Nicole.

"Just trying to help," she said with a forced sweetness.

"Auntie Nicole did help," Tristan said looking up from his work. "The house was almost burning down, but then Auntie Nicole pulled the yucky casserole out of the oven—"

"And Auntie Isabelle was supposed to watch it," Justin interrupted. "She forgot because she was on the phone and then we had to help Auntie Nicole wave at the detector."

"You little tattletale," Isabelle snapped, slamming another bowl onto the drying rack.

"It's true. You were talking on the phone and Gramma couldn't sleep 'cause the detector went off," Justin said, his face growing red. "I'm not a tattletale."

"You are," Isabelle retorted.

"I'm not. You're a tattler. All you do is tattle on the phone."

"You better watch yourself, mister," Isabelle said.

"I think we're done here," Nicole said, flashing Isabelle a warning look. "Unless you want to continue an argument with a five-year-old?"

Isabelle blew out a sigh, but to Kip's surprise, said nothing more.

Nicole pulled Justin off the counter, then slowly pulled off her apron. "And I'd better be going."

Kip wasn't proud that he felt relieved. She'd made supper, brought order to the chaos that had been the kitchen, yet he was glad that she wasn't sticking around. Besides not being a friend to this family, she was starting to slip into his thoughts the times she wasn't here.

"What? No. You can't. You have to stay." His mother and the twins all spoke at once.

"Ms. Williams probably has business to get to," Kip added.

"Of course you have to stay for supper," Mary protested. "If it wasn't for you we'd be eating peanut butter sandwiches." Kip's mother turned to him, frowning. "Kip, make her stay."

Kip glanced from his mother to the boys, feeling outnumbered.

"Please stay," he said to Nicole, relenting. "I appreciate what you did for us here."

Nicole slowly folded the apron she'd been wearing. "You don't have to go through the motions for me," she said quietly.

The thought of her going back to an empty motel room bothered him.

"No. Really," he said, projecting some warmth into his voice. "Please stay. It's the least we can do for all your help. You made dinner. You should at least stay around to eat it."

Nicole's smile shifted and she angled her head to one side as if studying him. "Thanks for that. I believe I will stay."

Five minutes later everyone was gathered around the table. Nicole sat directly across from Kip, the twins flanking her. Usually they sat beside him, but the boys had scooted over to her side when she sat down.

He felt a pang as he watched them take her hands before they prayed. She smiled down at them and the picture eased sorrow into his heart.

They would never remember their mother. Though they had grown up with his mother and his sister in their lives, it wasn't the same.

He wished again that things were different for the boys. He wished again that he could give them all the things they missed out on.

Which made him wonder when he should tell them about their mother. An opportunity hadn't come up, and he didn't want Nicole to be the one to tell them.

Just at that moment Nicole looked up at him. Their gazes met and a peculiar awareness rose up. It was as tangible as a touch, and it not only surprised him, it rocked him. He looked down, not sure where to put feelings he had neither space nor time for. Feelings for a woman whose plans had the potential to throw his life into turmoil.

Kip cleared his throat, pulling himself back to reality. "We usually pray before our meals."

He lowered his head, waited a moment while he shifted his focus. He never spent enough time in concentrated prayer. Too often his prayers were a hurried, please, please. Or an equally rushed, thank you, thank you.

But at mealtime, he had an opportunity to slow down, at least for a few moments, and make his prayer sincere.

"Thank you, Lord for our food. For the hands that prepared it." His thoughts slipped to Nicole as he hesitated. While he was thankful for what she did, he still struggled with her presence in their lives and what might happen. He pushed on, determined not to let her dominate his life right now. "Thank You for the lives You give us and the many blessings we have. Thank You for each other. Help us to be a blessing to this family. Help us to use our gifts, our time and our lives for You. Be with us this evening. Help us to trust You in every part of our life." Help me to trust that you didn't bring the boys into our lives just to take them away, he added quietly. "All this we ask in Jesus' name, Amen."

He waited a moment, then lifted his head. Justin and Tristan began talking right away, as they usually did, but Nicole was looking across the table at him again. Her forehead held the faintest of frowns. As if she was trying to figure him out.

"I hope you like quiche," Isabelle said to Kip, her voice dripping with disdain. "Because that's what Ms. Williams made us for supper."

He wasn't crazy about it, but he wasn't about to diss food that he didn't make himself.

"Looks good," Kip said, serving up his mother.

"What is this stuff?" Justin asked, poking his quiche with his fork. "It looks gross."

"Justin, you know we don't use that word when we talk about food." Kip shot him a warning frown to underline his reprimand.

"I like it," Tristan said, taking a big mouthful. "It's really good."

"I still think it's gross." Justin leaned back in his chair, his chin resting on his chest.

"Justin, what did I say?" Kip warned. The boy had been pushing his patience the past few days. It was as if he understood on some level the tension between him and Nicole.

Justin stared back at him, then his lower lip quivered. "I don't want to eat. My stomach hurts and I miss my dad."

Kip's anger left him like air out of a balloon. "Oh, Justin," he said, his own sorrow sliding into his voice. "Come here, buddy."

Justin slipped off his chair and walked over to Kip. Kip pulled the little boy up onto his lap and held him close. "I'm sorry, buddy. I wish I could make it better," he murmured, wrapping his arms tightly around his nephew.

He looked over at Tristan, who was still eating as if he hadn't even noticed Justin's little breakdown. Kip often wondered how could two boys could look so alike and yet be so different.

Justin was all drama and noise, just like Scott could be, and Tristan was quieter and more sedate. Which made him wonder what Tricia was like.

His gaze drifted over just enough to catch Nicole watching him. Her fingers rested lightly on her lips, as if holding back the glimpse of sorrow he caught in her eyes. Then she blinked and looked away and the moment was gone.

Justin sat quiet a moment, then sniffed. "Do I still have to eat my quiche?"

Kip sighed, feeling as if he had been played by his nephew. He wasn't sure what to say, but before he could speak his mother touched Justin on the arm.

"No, you don't, honey. I'll make you something else when dinner's over."

"Mom, you shouldn't…" but then he stopped himself. He didn't have the energy to deal with this.

"If Justin doesn't have to eat his quiche, do I?" Isabelle asked hopefully.

Kip shot her an annoyed glance. She got the hint and resumed poking at her supper with her fork.

"I'm sorry," Nicole said quietly. "I thought quiche would be safe."

"It is," Kip said. "We haven't eaten it a lot." Juggling Justin on his lap he took another bite.

It tasted a bit better now that he knew what to expect.

"You should try a bite, Justin," he encouraged. "It tastes really good."

Justin lifted his head and with a sigh took an offered bite. He ate it, then laid his head down on Kip's chest again. Kip didn't mind. His nephews were getting more independent every day, so he enjoyed the moments when they needed him.

"She made this out of her head," his mother told him. "I watched her."

"I like cooking," Nicole offered. "I often helped our cook make meals."

"You had a cook?" Isabelle asked. "You must be rich."

Kip had wondered himself about Nicole's financial situation. Having a personal cook definitely put her beyond his financial situation.

"We had a cook, yes, and I liked helping her."

"If I was rich I wouldn't help cook," Isabelle continued. "Of course the only way I might get rich is to move off this ranch."

"What do you want to do when you're finished high school?" Nicole asked.

Isabelle tossed her hair. "Be an actress. See the world."

"Do you take drama in school?" Nicole asked, reaching across to help Tristan with the last of his supper.

"I wish. They don't offer it in my school."

"That's too bad. It's always helpful to get a taste of what you want to do when you're young." Nicole turned her attention back to Justin. "Do you want to try some of your own supper? It tastes the same as your uncle's."

Justin lifted his head and looked across the table at Nicole, then to Kip's surprise, he slipped off Kip's lap and scooted around the table to Nicole.

Kips wished Nicole had left Justin be. Soon enough the little boy wouldn't want to sit on his uncle's lap.

"So where in Toronto do you live?" Kip's mother asked Nicole.

"My father has a home in Rosedale."

"Where's that?" Isabelle asked.

"Rich part of Toronto," Kip said. "Lot's of walls and gated yards."

"Did you live all your life in Toronto area?" Mary asked, ignoring Kip's jibe.

"My parents did." Nicole's smile tightened. "I was born in Winnipeg, Manitoba."

Kip was puzzled. "So your parents moved—"

"Sam and Norah Williams are my adoptive parents," Nicole said. "I grew up…spent the first years of my life in, uh, foster homes."

"Oh, I'm sorry to hear that," Mary said, sympathy lacing her voice. "Was that difficult?"

Nicole lifted her shoulder in a delicate shrug.

"I was blessed to be taken in by the Williamses when I was eight. They've been very good to me and I owe them more than I can ever repay."

Her voice faltered, and as Kip witnessed the faint break in her defenses he felt a nudge of sympathy that was both unexpected and unwelcome. He didn't want to feel sorry for her.

It was easier to deal dispassionately with her if he could see her simply as an opponent. Bad enough that she had come into his house and blurred the lines.

"I'm done," Justin announced, shoveling more food into his mouth. The little boy's stomach couldn't be that sore, Kip thought.

"Good. You're the last one," Nicole said, getting up. "Now we can do the dishes."

"If you don't mind, Nicole, we often have devotions after supper," Kip said. "The dishes might have to wait a bit."

She immediately sat down, looking a bit flustered. "Oh. I see. I'm sorry."

"Tristan, can you get me the Bible?"

Tristan was already out of his chair. The two boys took turns getting the Bible and sitting on his lap while he read, and today it was Tristan's turn.

Tristan handed him the Bible but returned to Nicole's side, which bothered Kip more than he cared to admit.

"We've been reading through Matthew," Kip said, turning to the passage. He cleared his throat, and as he read he felt Nicole's eyes on him. He had a hard time concentrating, but then he reminded himself that he was reading God's Holy Word and let the words become part of him. "Come to me, all you who are weary and burdened, and I will give you rest. Take my yoke upon you and learn from me, for I am gentle and humble in heart, and you will find rest for your souls. For my yoke is easy and my burden is light." Kip stopped as the words resonated in his mind. *You will find rest for your souls'.* He lowered his head and began praying. He asked that he could learn to put all his cares and concerns in God's loving hands.

When he was done, he glanced up to see Nicole staring at him, her brow holding a faint frown.

"Can we take Auntie Nicole to see the puppies again?" Justin begged.

"We'll have to do the dishes first," Nicole said.

"After the dishes." Justin turned to Kip. "Can we? Please?"

"I don't think that's a good idea," Kip said, remembering the last time she'd taken the boys to see the puppies. Though he hadn't been proud of his reaction—part of it was plain and simple fear—he still believed he was right to insist she run anything new past him first.

Nicole glanced over at him, an enigmatic look on her face. It was as if she knew exactly what he was thinking.

"I have to call Nellie back," Isabelle announced, pushing back from the table.

"Before you do that, can you help me clear the dishes?" Nicole asked, getting up.

Isabelle shot her a puzzled frown as if wondering who this woman was who was asking her favors. She sent Kip a look of appeal.

"That's okay, Nicole. I don't mind helping," his mother said.

"See? Mom can help," Isabelle said with a triumphant note in her voice and a faint sneer in Nicole's direction.

He sighed, feeling as if he was stuck between a sister who was basically lazy and a mother who enabled her. Though Kip understood why Isabelle would resent taking orders from a woman she barely knew, at the same time he was disappointed that his little sister couldn't see that their mother wasn't able to help much.

Then he caught Nicole looking at him, as if wondering what he was going to do and he stiffened his back.

"Mom, you go into the living room and watch television," he said, coming up with his own solution. "Isabelle, you can make your phone call but keep it short. I'll do the dishes."

"Can we help you and Auntie Nicole do dishes too?" Justin and Tristan asked, their eyes lighting up.

"Of course you can," Nicole said, bringing a stack of plates to the kitchen counter.

Nicole got the boys clearing the table while she walked over to the counter, pulled on her apron again and started cleaning up.

"As you can see we don't have a dishwasher." He didn't know why he was apologizing for the lack.

"No big deal." She started running water in the sink and getting the boys to find some dry dish towels.

He returned to the table and pulled off the tablecloth, not sure what to do with it. "And where did you find this?"

"Isabelle found it in your mother's bedroom," Nicole said, shooting him a quick glance over her shoulder. "I hope that was okay."

She added a gentle smile to the glance and again their gazes tangled. She didn't turn her head away and for a moment, neither did he.

Don't be an idiot, he told himself, breaking the connection. *You're just a lonely bachelor, that's all.*

He folded up the tablecloth with jerky movements. "That a rich Toronto thing? A tablecloth on the table?" That came out a bit more harsh than he intended. Truth was she made him uncomfortable and he had to keep things impersonal.

Of course having her in his kitchen, wearing his mother's apron after making his family supper didn't exactly create an impersonal atmosphere.

"Actually it is. All the very wealthy people use tablecloths," she snapped.

He'd made her mad. Well, that was his intention, wasn't it?

With every visit and everything she did for him and for his family, she seemed to be slowly seeping into his life.

And the trouble was, part of him didn't mind. She was helpful, capable.

And attractive.

You can't afford to go there, he reminded himself. She's trouble.

He set the folded tablecloth on the worn wooden table, noticing again how old and scarred it was. He and his brother and sisters had grown up around this table, arguing and bickering over doing the dishes, doing chores and whatever else it was that siblings argued about.

Until half a year ago, his brother sat here as well.

Kip clenched his fist, willing away the memories, forcing himself to the present. He looked over his shoulder again at Nicole, who was teasing Justin and encouraging Tristan.

And this woman, standing in his kitchen, was part of the present he didn't want to deal with.

"Weeding the garden? You sure you know which ones to pull?"

Kip's voice made Nicole look up. All she saw of him was his outline silhouetted against the blue sky. He looked larger than life and, as he had the past couple of days, the sight of him lifted her heart. Being around him gave her the tiniest thrill.

It's the whole rugged-man thing that he carries off so well with his piercing gaze and smoldering looks, she thought, trying to pull back and analyze her reaction.

And let's not forget the cowboy hat.

Yet even as she tried to be casual about it, she knew there was more to his appeal than simply looks.

"I go by height," she said airily, trying to dismiss her reaction to him. "If it's tall and healthy-looking, I figure it must be a weed."

"Gramma is helping," Justin said, pointing to his grandmother, who sat on a bench at the end of the garden overseeing the operation. "She's telling us what to pull."

Nicole glanced over the mat of green tangled plants. "It's an ongoing battle," she said.

"The curse of the earth," Kip replied. "Adam had to deal with it from the beginning."

"So why are we doing this instead of you?"

Kip laughed, then reached over and yanked out a large-leafed plant. Pigweed, Mary had told her. "Because I'm tilling the ground on a different scale."

"At least you get to use a tractor."

"Air-conditioned, too," he added, pointing to a bead of sweat working its way down her temple.

She hurriedly wiped it away, suddenly self-conscious. Usually when she was talking to men she wore a suit, her hair was pinned back and she had an attitude. Usually she was in charge. Not on her knees with dirt under her nails and probably smears on her face.

In spite of that, she knew she felt more comfortable than she'd had around any man she'd met in a while.

It was a distraction she couldn't afford. She had her own plans, the culmination of which would mean her leaving with the boys he claimed were Cosgroves. That leaving would effectively kill any hint of attraction she sensed growing between them.

And why did that bother her?

"Have you ever done any gardening before?" Kip asked.

"The closest my mother came to having a garden was when I brought home a bean plant in grade six."

"In a foam cup too, I'm sure."

Nicole laughed. "You too?"

"I think it's a classic." He pulled another weed and tossed it aside. "So you know what a bean plant looks like."

"I don't know if I can think back that far." She moved forward a bit more and reached for another weed just as he did. Their hands brushed each other and she jerked hers back.

And now you're acting like you're back in grade six again.

He sat back on his heels. "I have a couple of favors to ask," he said. "Tomorrow I promised a buddy that I would go help him do some welding, so would you mind watching the boys?"

"So you won't be around?" she said. This would be a treat for her, not having him around.

"Nope. Sorry. I know you'll miss me like crazy, but a guy's gotta do what a guy's gotta do."

Nicole couldn't help a chuckle at that. "Noble of you. But no, I don't mind." It was on the tip of her tongue to ask him if she could take them to town, but she thought she could save that for another time.

He pulled out another weed, then pushed himself to his feet and walked over to his mother.

"Good to see you out here," she heard Kip say to his mother, walking over to her side. "How are you feeling?"

"A lot better. Nicole convinced me that I'd feel better if I went outside and she was right."

"That's great," Kip said. "I better get back to work. Didn't get as much done yesterday as I hoped."

"You got the fence fixed and went out on Duke," Mary said. "You haven't had a chance to go riding in months."

"Nope. I haven't. Duke was a bit out of shape."

Nicole heard the longing in his voice. She wasn't surprised. This morning Mary had told her that Kip used to practically live with the horses before Scott died.

Then she had given Nicole a bright smile. "Thanks to you taking care of the boys, he's able to go now," she had said. Then Mary had launched into further stories from the past. How Kip, an A-plus scholar, had dropped out of school when his father died so he could take care of the ranch and his mother and Isabelle.

Nicole had heard about all the work Kip took on when Scott left and how Scott had returned to the ranch with the two boys, which only made more work for him. How Kip provided for them all and how he worried about the financial well-being of the ranch.

Mary showed Nicole pictures of Kip, but the one that stood out the most was a picture that had been taken when he won at the Ponoka stampede. The photographer caught him standing on the chuck wagon, leaning forward, reins threaded through his hands as he urged his horses on.

She saw, through the pictures and Mary's stories, a side of Kip that she wasn't sure she wanted to get to know. It was a side of him that created a mixture of sadness and admiration for the sacrifices he had made for his family and for the boys.

Nicole knew she was in danger of seeing Kip as human. Caring. Compassionate.

Trouble.

"Do you think you'll have a chance to enter a team in any of the races?" she heard Mary asking Kip.

"Those times are over, Mom," Kip said with a note of finality that made Nicole think back to the pictures.

She stopped her thoughts, but even as she did, she chanced another look up. Kip was looking directly at her.

She couldn't decipher his expression and wasn't sure she wanted to spend much time trying to figure him out.

She dragged her attention back to the gardening. She had to make another phone call to her father's lawyer. Surely something had to have happened by now.

She didn't want to stay here any longer than she had to.

Chapter Nine

"How are things between you and the cowboy?" Heather asked.

Nicole tucked the phone under her ear and sat down at the minuscule table that passed for a desk in her motel room. "And a good morning to you, too," Nicole said to her assistant.

"Sorry. Good morning back. I've been hanging around your dad too long," Heather said with a laugh. "I tend to get straight to the point."

"May as well, there's a lot to do. As for the cowboy, we've agreed to disagree," was all she said, preferring not to talk about Kip.

Yesterday he had been at his friend's place doing some welding, and today he'd been busy with the horses, which meant he wanted Justin and Tristan out of the way.

She had been only too happy to oblige. Being around Kip confused her and frustrated her.

"Your father's been putting major pressure on me to pressure you to find out what's happening with the boys," Heather said.

"I don't have anything to report." Last week this would have frustrated Nicole, but part of her didn't mind the time she spent with the boys without her father around.

"This cowboy of yours. Will he give up the boys or will it get down to a battle?"

"He's not my cowboy, and even though we've come to a bit of a truce now, when push comes to shove it will be a fight." Nicole rubbed her forehead, not sure she wanted to imagine her and Kip in that situation. "He's attached to the boys and they're attached to him."

"Of course they would be. They spent most of their life with him. No thanks to his brother taking the boys away."

Nicole felt the same way, yet each day she was at the ranch gave her more insight into Kip's life, gave her a bit more knowledge of him as a person.

Made her more attracted to him.

"By the way, I stopped in at your place. Did you know your dad is fixing up Tricia's old room for the boys?"

A shiver danced down Nicole's spine. Tricia's room hadn't been touched or changed since she left all those years ago. It was left like a shrine, as if waiting for her return.

"I suppose that's a good sign. It means he's moving on." At the same time it created an extra layer of pressure that Nicole couldn't deal with yet.

"I may as well warn you, your father is doing more than fixing up the room. He's got me checking out private-detective agencies."

"That seems a bit extreme."

"Nothing else is happening. Your dad's lawyer seems to be stalling out and your dad's getting antsy." Heather sighed, and Nicole was fairly sure her assistant was on the receiving end of some of her father's frustration. "Change of subject," Nicole said abruptly. "I'm still waiting for a quote from the caterer, and the venue's been making noises about an increase in costs. I'm looking into a few alternatives just to keep them on their toes."

"You do realize that I'm perfectly capable of doing that," Heather reprimanded.

"I've got to do something while I'm waiting for visits."

"I'll call the lawyer again and put more pressure on him, and you should stop worrying about the fund-raiser. I do have some experience with this."

Nicole knew that, but the fund-raiser was a major source of income and prestige for the foundation. And the foundation was her father's passion, the only way he could keep the memory of his beloved wife alive. Nicole's work for the foundation was one of the ways she had found she could maintain a connection to her father.

"You just develop some kind of relationship with those boys," Heather said, "so it's not such a shock to them when they come here. I'll take care of what I can over here."

Nicole was reassured by the authority in Heather's voice. Not *if* the boys come back, *when* they come back.

Nicole said goodbye, then got up and walked over to the window. From here, all she could see was the parking lot of the hardware store beside the motel. If she stepped outside, she could see the sun setting behind the mountains beyond the town, and for the faintest moment she felt a longing to go back to the farm that had nothing to do with the boys.

But she couldn't. Things were shifting between her and Kip. Her loyalties were getting strained. She had to get back in control of the situation. Starting now.

She picked up the phone and dialed.

Kip answered on the first ring and she plunged in.

"I'd like to take the boys to the Calgary Stampede tomorrow," she said.

Silence followed her request. She chafed at the pause, feeling like she was a minion begging for favors. The boys were as much hers as Kip's. Even though Tricia was her adopted sister, she was still her sister.

"What time would you be coming for them?" he asked.

Nicole was taken aback. She thought he would fight her on this. "I was hoping to pick them at eleven and spend the day at the Stampede, then take them on the midway."

"That's more than the usual time," he said.

"I think I'm due a bit more than the 'usual time,'" she replied with some asperity, trying to create some distance.

"I suppose you are. What time did you figure on being back?"

"I hope to be back by nine o'clock in the evening. Of course that would depend on traffic and anything else out of my control." She didn't mean to sound snappy. She didn't like feeling like a potential date being grilled by a suspicious parent.

This netted her another thoughtful pause on his end. She heard his muffled conversation. What could he possibly have to think about or consult his family about? It was a simple yes or no answer.

"Okay. That might work," he said when he came back to the phone. "I'll see you tomorrow."

Nicole heard a click in her ear and then she stared at the phone. Well. I guess that was that. Tomorrow she was taking the boys out. All by herself. She smiled at the thought, but behind that came the tiniest touch of regret.

It would have been kind of fun if Kip came along.

She pushed that thought aside. She had been thinking about him too much lately. Time to focus on what lay ahead.

Bringing the boys back.

Saturday morning dawned with a spill of bright sunshine and a clear blue sky. Nicole smiled as she drove to the ranch, thinking of her day alone with Justin and Tristan. She was looking forward to a break from the tension of constantly being around Kip and his family. She needed to feel like the boys were hers. Needed to spend some time one-on-one with them.

When she pulled into the ranch yard, the familiar sight of the house nestled against the tree-covered hills rolling upward to the mountains created anticipation.

She was going to see the boys, her boys, again.

As always a small part of her held back committing all her emotions. People left, she knew.

When she stepped out of the car and the boys came barreling down the stairs toward her, however, she ignored her innate wariness, bent over and pulled them into her arms and into her heart.

They smelled like hay. "Have you been helping your Uncle Kip haul hay again?" she asked, pulling back.

"We were playing on the bales," Justin reported. "Uncle Kip had to do some welding so he didn't want us around."

"That's good thinking." Nicole pulled out a handkerchief and wiped a smear of jam from the corner of Justin's mouth. "Looks like you had lunch already," she said with a touch of disappointment. She had hoped to get them something to eat at the Stampede.

"Just enough to take the edge off," Tristan said. "At least that's what Gramma told me."

"Great. Now you boys stay here inside my car and don't move an inch. I want to say hi to your gramma, and when I come back we're going."

She buckled the boys in, then fairly flew up the stairs. She was going to have so much fun. She was going to spoil these boys absolutely rotten.

Then, just as she stepped onto the verandah, the door opened and Kip stood before her. He wore a clean shirt that she remembered Mary folding the first day she had come. The day they thought she was the housekeeper.

His blue jeans were crisply new and he had shaved, making him look less gruff and more approachable. His hair, still damp from a shower, curled over his forehead and around his ears. He looked even more appealing than he usually did.

Nicole pushed down her reaction and forced herself not to take a step back. "I want to say hello to your mother," she said, hating the breathless tone in her voice. "I'll just be a minute, then I'll be leaving." She ducked around him, catching a whiff of laundry soap and aftershave. She wondered where he was headed. A date? But he was always talking about how busy he was.

Why do you care?

Nicole pushed open the door of the porch and stepped into the house.

Mary Cosgrove stood by the sink, leaning on her walker with one arm, doing dishes with her free hand. It looked awkward and uncomfortable and Nicole had to resist the urge to help her. But she was glad to see her up and about.

"Hey, Mary. I've come to say hello," Nicole said.

Mary glanced up and a welcoming smile. "Well, that's kind of you. As you can see, I'm using my walker."

"That's great." Nicole frowned as Mary washed another plate one-handed. "Where's Isabelle?"

"She's in the bathroom."

Tricia used to do that, Nicole thought. Her little sister could make a bathroom break stretch out long enough to miss loading the dishwasher and cleaning up the kitchen. Her mother always let her get away with it.

"She can easily help you," Nicole said, regretting the sharp tone her voice took.

"I know," Mary said with a gentle sigh. "It's less work to do the dishes myself than it is to make her help me."

"Kip should be helping you out."

Mary frowned. "Kip doesn't have to do the dishes. He works hard enough on the ranch."

"I meant with Isabelle," Nicole replied.

Mary shrugged. "I don't think he always knows what to do with her either."

Nicole bit back another reply, realizing that all this badgering and pushing was none of her business.

"Well, I'm leaving with the boys. You take care," Nicole said quietly. Then she left before she could offer more of her unneeded advice. The Cosgroves' problems weren't hers, she reminded herself as she closed the door of the house behind her.

The unmistakable growl of Kip's truck resonated through the quiet. Guess he was off on his date now that he didn't have to watch the twins.

She squinted against the sun then lifted her hand to shade her eyes as she looked at her car. Empty.

"Justin. Tristan. Where are you?" she called, walking toward her car, her gaze flickering over the yard. She was so sure she had told them to stay put.

Then she heard the honk of a horn and saw Justin leaning out the back window of Kip's truck, waving at her.

What in the world was going on? And where did Kip Cosgrove think he was going with the boys?

She marched over to the driver's window and as she did, Kip rolled it down.

"I thought it would be better if we took my truck. There's more room for all of us than in that car you're driving."

"What…how…" she sputtered, trying to comprehend what he was saying.

"I'm coming along," he announced pushing his cowboy hat back on his head.

Anger washed over her. She didn't want to share her time with the boys. Especially not with him.

"C'mon, Auntie Nicole. Let's go," Tristan said, leaning out of the back window. "We don't want to miss anything."

She felt suddenly impotent, unable to speak openly in front of the boys, her own feelings a tangle of mixed emotions. She grabbed onto her anger, suspecting she would need it as a defense. "I understood the boys and I were going alone…"

Kip shrugged. "You understood wrong. Are you coming? It's a long drive. Don't want to waste any time." His steady gaze held hers and she read resolute determination.

Nicole tried to hold her ground as various emotions danced through her head. Anger, yes, but behind that a vague hungering for a chance to spend more time with this man.

She truncated that thought. She and Kip could never be anything but adversaries.

"I'll get my purse."

Ten minutes later the truck's tires hummed on the asphalt, a country song whined from the radio and the boys narrated the trip from the backseat.

"Mr. and Mrs. Ogilvie live there," Justin said. "Last year when Isabelle took us out trick-or-treating, we got four chocolate bars from them. They were yummy. But Mr. Jorritsma always has the best candy and he brings honey to the farmers' market."

They told her about trips to see friends, play dates with cousins and how cute Auntie Doreen's brand-new baby was.

The plus of all that chatter was that Nicole didn't have to say anything to Kip.

So she formed her lips into a smile and nodded, listening to the boys, all the while pretending not to be fully aware of the tall figure sitting behind the wheel. He steered one-handed, the other resting on the open window as he drove, looking as comfortable as if he were lounging on a couch watching television.

She wished she felt as comfortable. She had hoped to avoid him today, but they sat mere feet from each other, and with each mile her anger seemed more foolish. He was here. He wasn't going away. May as well enjoy her time with the boys.

"So what did you boys do this morning?" she asked, half turning in the seat so she could focus on them.

"Uncle Kip got up real, real early," Justin said.

"He said he wanted to get done on time 'cause he had a hot date." Tristan frowned. "What's a hot date?"

She couldn't stop a quick glance Kip's way. He was rolling his eyes and a flush warmed her cheeks. She wasn't sure she wanted to know exactly what Kip meant by that. Sarcasm, most likely.

"I think it means that the day was going to be warm," Nicole said, letting him off the hook.

"And he was whistling, even though he had to get up early and work on the stupid welder," Tristan added.

"You don't need to say that," Kip said with a note of reprimand.

"That's what you called it."

"I shouldn't have, okay?"

"Radioactive hearing," Nicole murmured, shooting Kip a quick glance.

He shrugged. "I've got to learn to keep my big mouth shut."

She suspected he was referring to his previous comment but wasn't sure she wanted to analyze that too much.

"Have you been to Stampede?" Justin asked, unbuckling his seatbelt.

"No. I've never been, and what do you think you're doing?"

"Justin, get back in your seat and buckle up," Kip said at exactly the same time.

We sound like parents, Nicole thought, forcing herself to keep looking at her nephew.

Justin glanced from Nicole to Kip as if trying to figure this arrangement out.

"Justin—"

"Now—"

"Okay, okay. You both don't have to be so bossy."

Nicole was about to reprimand him again, but held back in case Kip had the same idea. At least when it came to the boys' safety, they agreed.

"I'm bored," Justin grumbled after he buckled up.

"Then let's play a driving game. We can play I Spy."

"How do you play that?" Tristan asked.

Nicole explained the rules and soon they were guessing all kinds of things from the feather in the hatband of Uncle Kip's cowboy hat to the pattern stitched into their little cowboy boots to the color of Nicole's eyes.

"I think they're blue," Tristan said, leaning forward as if to get a better look.

"Nuh-uh. Gray," Justin announced.

"What color are they, Auntie Nicole?" Tristan asked.

"I don't know. One of my foster mothers said they were the color of dishwater," Nicole said with a light laugh. She didn't really want to talk about her eyes. Not with Kip sitting next to her, smiling and glancing at her from time to time as if trying to decide for himself on their color.

"What's a foster mother?" Justin asked.

Trust him not to miss the slightest slip of the tongue, Nicole thought.

"A foster mother is someone who takes care of children when they can't live at their own place," Nicole said with a smile. "Now it's my turn. I spy with my little eye—"

"You said you had foster mothers," Justin interrupted. "How many did you have?"

"Doesn't matter how many—"

"How could you have more than one? Didn't you have your own mother?"

"My mother died when I was very little," Nicole said. "So I went to live with another family—"

"Didn't your dad take care of you?" Tristan asked.

"My father...was a busy man. He was gone a lot."

"Did your dad miss you when he was gone?" Justin asked.

Nicole wasn't sure how to answer that question. She often wondered herself. Her father never seemed excessively eager to return to her, and when he did come it was usually a brief appearance, then he was gone again.

"I hope he did," she said quietly.

"Where did you live when he was gone?" Justin asked.

"I lived with my auntie for a while."

"Was she a foster mom?"

Nicole wished they would get off this topic already so she simply said yes.

"But you had lots of foster moms."

They weren't going to quit. She sighed and knew she had to give them the entire rundown.

"I lived with my auntie for a while, and when my dad died and she couldn't take care of me anymore she put me in a foster home. When they couldn't take care of me anymore, they put me in another one. Then I got adopted by the Williams family. So that's my story. Now why don't you tell me yours?" she said. Though she knew it well, she wanted to stop talking about her past. It was over and done with, thanks to Sam and Norah Williams.

Besides, she didn't like the way Kip was looking at her. The faint frown on his face as if he was trying to figure out what to think of her now that he knew more about her past.

"Our dad died too," Justin said. "But he took care of us all the time and so did Uncle Kip."

"You had lots of mothers and had lots of fathers but we have a mommy and we don't know where she is," Tristan said, a gentle sadness entering his voice.

Nicole didn't want to look at Kip, knowing they were both thinking about Tricia and when they should tell the boys, but at the same time, like a magnetic force, their eyes met. In his gaze she saw concern and, at the same time, an indefinable emotion that called to her loneliness.

She tore her gaze away as she struggled to be analytical about the situation. He was a single, attractive man. She was a single woman. They were spending a lot of time together. So something was bound to happen.

"Uncle Kip used to race chuck wagons, but he doesn't anymore. He gots trophies. Lots of trophies."

"Can we watch the chuck-wagon races tonight, Uncle Kip?" Justin asked, suddenly excited.

Kip shrugged and shot another glance at Nicole. "I don't know if Nicole is interested."

"I've never seen a chuck-wagon race," she said. "It sounds very exciting."

"We'll see." Then Kip straightened, his attention focussed on his driving as they entered Calgary. The traffic got busier and he turned off the radio, and soon they were hemmed in by vehicles all racing toward the next traffic light. They made their way slowly up the McLeod Trail. Though Nicole travelled in traffic when she lived in Toronto, she found the sudden busyness disconcerting and, surprisingly, annoying.

Funny how used she had gotten to driving quiet roads from the motel to the ranch and how much she enjoyed it. Well, she'd have to get used to traffic soon enough when she and the boys moved back to Toronto.

After numerous intersections and hundreds of vehicles, Kip pulled off into a huge parking lot and drove around until he finally found an empty spot big enough for the truck.

Nicole got out before he even had the truck turned off and was opening the back door to let the boys out. Tristan was already unbuckled and he jumped into her outstretched arms. Justin, however, went to Kip.

As Nicole walked around the truck she heard the squeal of people, the pounding music from some of the rides and the general hubbub emitted by fairgrounds the world over. She felt a peculiar sense of anticipation. She'd been to a fair only once in her life.

"Before we go any farther, I have to say something to you boys." Kip caught the boys by the hand and knelt down so that he was face to face with them. "We're going to a very busy place. You have to remember to stay close. You're not to run off. You have to be holding either Nicole's or my hand. Do you understand?"

They both nodded.

"Do you both understand?" he repeated again.

"Yes. We do," they both said again.

"Okay, then, as long as that's clear, let's go."

Tristan grabbed Nicole's hand, Justin caught Kip's and then the boys held each others, anchoring the adults.

Just like a family.

Nicole wanted to push the thought aside, but at the same time, she was tired of juggling her feelings. Trying to ignore her attraction to Kip and her appreciation of who he was.

This was supposed to be a fun time, and she intended to enjoy herself. This was like a little holiday. She wasn't thinking past today. She was with a good-looking man and she was free from responsibilities for the day.

Why not simply enjoy it?

Chapter Ten

It had been years since he'd been to Stampede. Everywhere Kip looked he saw cowboy hats, blue jeans and cowboy boots. Most were the brand-new hats of the once-a-year cowboys, but a lot were well-worn. The tinny sounds of carousels and blaring music from busy rides mingled with the oily scent of funnel cakes and hot dogs.

Though he'd crawled out of bed at some ridiculous hour so he could get done with the farm work on time, it was worth every minute of lack of sleep to see the looks of wonder on the boys' faces as they stood in the center of this milling crowd.

He glanced over at Nicole, who was glancing around with a bemused look on her face. He thought of her comments in the truck and wondered how many fairs she'd been to in her life. He doubted very many.

Though she'd spoken quietly and unemotionally

about her past, Kip had sensed a hidden pain and sorrow that made him see her through different eyes. Her life hadn't been so privileged after all.

"So where do we start?" Nicole asked.

"For now we just wander around, and take it all in."

"We should buy Auntie Nicole a cowboy hat," Tristan said.

"I don't know if Auntie Nicole can pull off a cowboy hat." Kip glanced at Nicole's distressed blue jeans and silk shirt.

"I chased cows the other day," Nicole protested. "I think I'm a good candidate for a cowboy hat."

"I don't know if that's enough of a qualification," he said, responding to her humor.

"I also know how to ride a horse," she said with another grin as she stepped aside to avoid a man pushing a baby buggy.

"And you probably ride English," Kip said, giving Tristan's hand a bit of a tug, reminding him to stay close.

"It's not as easy as it looks," she replied.

"Auntie Nicole should ride the horses at the ranch," Tristan said, jumping with excitement. "Then we can too."

Kip shook his head. "I don't think so, buddy."

Nicole shot him a puzzled glance, and though he wasn't about to elaborate, he got the feeling that sometime or another she would ask him more about it.

They wandered through the crowds and past rides, working their way to the events' barns. They turned a corner and came upon a group of people in a circle cheering on three children riding pedal tractors racing each other to a finish line.

When Justin saw this he tried to break free of Kip's hand. "Can we race? Please?"

Kip frowned as he looked over the crowd.

"I'm here too, you know," Nicole said.

"What do you mean?"

"I can watch the boys too." She added a crooked smile which made him wonder if she was teasing him just a bit.

He couldn't help but smile back. A relaxed Nicole was, he had to admit, fun to be around. "Okay. I guess it'll be fine."

"Goody." Justin grabbed Tristan's hand.

Kip let them go to stand in line while he and Nicole moved in closer. People walked around them and gathered ahead of them, yet Kip felt so aware of Nicole it was as if no one else existed.

"So tell me a bit about your chuck-wagon racing. Do you miss it?" Though her question was quiet, he sensed her sympathy.

"Yeah. I do." He let his mind slip back, pulling up memories and he smiled.

"What do you miss the most?"

"I don't know," he said, shrugging her question aside.

"You must miss something," she pressed.

Kip shot her a puzzled look. "Why does it matter?"

Nicole held his gaze for a moment, then looked away. "Because I'm guessing you gave it up for the boys, and…I think that's admirable and, well, I'd just like to know."

"Okay. Let's see." He scratched the side of his nose with his forefinger, trying to formulate his answer. No one had ever asked him what he missed, so he had to think a bit.

"I guess I miss the challenge and the thrill. The sound of the horn and then trying to jockey for first place after running the figure eight. The feel of those hooves thundering on the packed dirt and how you sense every shift of the horse in the reins, trying to read them and keep them working as a team." He stopped, feeling a touch of embarrassment at his enthusiasm. "That's in the past now."

"Still, it must have been hard to give up dreams," Nicole said quietly.

"Yeah. It was," he admitted. "Hanging around on the circuit gets expensive, and I need to think about the boys' financial future."

"I take it Scott had no life insurance?"

"Or a will." Something Nicole and her father did have granting them custody of the boys. Tricia

may have been irresponsible in some areas but not
in that one.

"I'm surprised Scott didn't ask your married sister to take Justin and Tristan," she said
quietly.

"Scott wanted the boys on the ranch, and my
sister was expecting a baby. I was too attached to
them to let the twins go anywhere else." He gave
her a careful smile, surprised to feel his reaction
to the softening of her features. A wayward breeze
tossed her hair, and a strand got caught in her lip
gloss.

Before he could stop himself, he reached over
and loosened her hair, his fingers lingering on her
cheek.

His heart gave a little thrum and he wondered,
just for a moment—

"We're going to race now," Tristan shouted
out.

Kip dragged his way emotions back to reality.
This was crazy. He had to keep his focus on the
boys.

The boys she was planning to take away.

Nicole followed Kip down the concrete stairs
of the arena to their seats, clinging to Tristan's
hand. The excited voices of people echoed in the
yawning space.

This was supposed to have been a time alone

with her and the boys, she thought, trying to work up her resentment. Kip wasn't supposed to be along.

The trouble was, the more time she spent with Kip, the more confused she grew. The more attracted she became to him.

Which definitely complicated her life. The purpose that had brought her here grew foggier with each day that she saw the boys with Kip and his family on the ranch.

This was the only life the boys had known. Could she really take them away from that?

She closed her eyes willing her mind to stop its ceaseless whirling and circling back. She was here with an attractive man experiencing something she could talk to her friends back home about once it was all over.

A date. Something she hadn't gone on for a while. So just enjoy it, she told herself.

"We're up in the nosebleed area, but we'll be able to see the whole track this way too," Kip said as they followed him to their seats. Below them lay a large open area surrounded by other bleachers and ringed by a racing track.

"I sit with Uncle Kip and Tristan sits with Auntie Nicole," Justin announced.

Auntie Nicole would have preferred to keep the boys between her and Kip, but the boys were already in their seats, leaving two open between them.

Just go with it, Nicole thought. Stop overthinking.

"So how does this race work?" she asked, determined to be casual about the situation.

"You see this space below us where the barrels are laid out?" Kip swept his hand over the large open area ringed by other, smaller bleachers. "That's where the first part of the race is. There's eight barrels, two for each team. The teams line up at a designated spot marked with chalk in the dirt, do a figure eight around each barrel in the open space, and then they have to head around the half mile track and come back to the finish line right below us."

"Looks complicated," Nicole said, trying to imagine what would happen.

"Then there's the four outriders," Kip added.

"What do they do?"

"They have to stay with the chuck wagons," Tristan said, clutching the teddy bear Kip had won for him in a shooting gallery.

"Each chuck wagon is assigned four outriders," Kip continued. "When the horn goes, they have to throw a stove and a couple of sticks into the back of the wagon, mount up and follow the chuck wagons through the pattern." Kip grew animated as he spoke, and he was grinning, leaning forward in his seat as if he could hardly wait for the races to start. "If they're too far behind their chuck wagon when he crosses the finish line, the team gets a penalty. Those outriders really give 'er to keep up."

Nicole was struggling as well to keep up, but she simply smiled and nodded, surprised at the excitement in Kip's voice.

"Here they come," he said, pointing to the track. Four teams of horses pulling what looked like a small covered wagon with wooden wheels came trotting down the track toward the place where other men were putting up the barrels.

"What's on the covers of the wagons?" Nicole asked.

"Sponsors' names. Costs a lot to keep a team of horses and a wagon racing in the circuit. Especially to get to the Stampede. Technically the chuck-wagon races are called the Rangeland Derby, but it's always part of Stampede." Kip clasped and unclasped his hands, his eyes tracking the movement of the chuck wagons. "Nick is here. Awesome." Kip shot her a quick grin. "Every time we competed he said he would quit, but he didn't and now he's here." He laughed, turning his attention back to the teams. "And Pete Nellisher. Huh. I never thought his team had it in them to get this far." The hunger in his voice was reflected in the expression on his face as he leaned forward.

He misses this more than he lets on, Nicole realized.

She remembered the smile of contentment on his face when he had come back from fixing the fences the day the cows got out.

He'd given up a lot to take care of the boys. She thought of the parked wagons and the dozens of horses the boys were supposed to stay away from. Kip made sacrifices that never came up in any conversation they'd ever had. From the way the boys talked, she knew they had no inkling of what he relinquished so he could be there for them. Kip could have easily left them with his mother every weekend. Could easily have carried on racing.

But he didn't. He gave all this up for the boys.

"See, each team has their starting position marked out," Kip said, leaning closer to her as he pointed to the teams moving into position. "This is one of the trickiest parts. See how antsy those horses are? They know what they have to do, but you have to make sure you get them to the starting position at exactly the right time. You get too close and they jump the horn. Too far and you lose valuable real estate." Kip's voice grew more intense, his full attention, like a laser, on the action below. He leaned closer to her, laying one hand on her shoulder, pointing with his other hand. "See how hard the guy at the head of the team has to work to keep the team back? The driver can't pull up too hard or the horses won't be ready."

A horn blared, Nicole jumped and Kip's hand dropped from her shoulder. He jerked forward as if the sound itself triggered an automatic reaction.

The outriders let go of the lead horses and jumped on their own, and soon the area around the barrels was a confusion of wagons and horses as four teams wove a figure eight.

"C'mon Nick, not too tight. Ease up. Ease up." Kip bit his lip, watching. "Yeah. Like that. Like that." He nodded his approval of his friend's work, inching to the edge of his seat. "See, Nicole, he's got to lean way over the side of the wagon to help the wagon move sideways. You've got to get into that inside lane right off the mark." He clasped his hands, nodding his approval of his friend's tactics. "Now lean left. Get those horses over to the inside. Lean. Lean," he yelled as his friend did exactly what Kip urged him to do. "Like that." He turned to Nicole, catching her hand in his. "He's doing it, he got the lead."

Nicole's attention was torn between the race and Kip's undivided attention to what was going on. He was more animated and alive than she'd ever seen him.

And his hand still clutched hers.

Then, when the racing wagons thundered around the last bend, outriders trailing behind the wagons, madly trying to keep up to their wagon, Kip jumped to his feet. "C'mon, Nick. C'mon."

Nick was standing up, leaning way ahead, urging the team on. He shot a glance over his shoulder as if to check where his outriders were, then he gave the horses another slap with the reins and they sailed across the finish line.

Kip hollered, waving his hat. "Yeah. Nick. Way to go."

Then Kip turned to her, grabbed her and gave her a bear hug, lifting her off the ground. "He won. Nick won." He pulled back, grinning and to her surprise and shock, planted a kiss on her mouth.

When he drew back, the astonishment Nicole felt was mirrored on Kip's face. For a moment they stared at each other, as if unsure of how to react or what to think.

Kip blew out his breath, then bent over to pick up his hat. "I'm...I'm sorry," he muttered. "I got carried away."

Nicole wished she could make a casual joke, but she was still trying to catch her breath. Trying to reorient herself.

Kip's kiss was unexpected but, to her surprise, not unwelcome.

"I was excited for your friend too." She drew in a quick breath, willing her heart to stop pounding.

"Did you give Auntie Nicole a kiss?" Tristan asked, his voice holding a teasing note.

"Shame, shame, double shame, now I know your girlfriend's name," Justin chanted in the sing-songy voice of the schoolyard.

Nicole ignored them as she sat down, her cheeks flushed and her heart beating erratically against her ribs.

It was the excitement of the moment, she reminded herself as the competitors trotted away, passing the next set of teams heading toward the starting position. The kiss was spontaneous and spur-of-the-moment…

And nothing like she'd ever experienced before.

Nicole folded her trembling hands together. She kept her eyes on the horses, but for the rest of the races, her attention was distracted by the man beside her.

Chapter Eleven

Chapter Eleven

That wasn't the dumbest thing he'd ever done, but it ranked right up there, Kip thought as he sat down. What had come over him, grabbing Nicole's hand like that? Kissing her like that?

It was the excitement of seeing his friend compete. Seeing him grab the lead, then win. That was all.

As awkwardness fell between him and Nicole. Kip knew his feelings and awareness of her were tied in with other factors. Her love for the boys even though she had just met them. The way she helped his mother, the way she handled herself with Isabelle.

Family was important to her. She was willing to do whatever it took to make her adoptive father happy and to bring her sister's boys back. Though this put her in opposition to him, her affection for the twins showed him a side of her that he respected and appreciated.

Justin poked Kip in the side. "Does kissing Auntie Nicole mean you love her?"

It means I'm an idiot, Kip thought.

"I was just excited to see Nick win," Kip said, shooting his nephew a warning glance. The teenager sitting beside Justin gave Kip a smirk as if he didn't believe him either.

"Why are you frowning?" Tristan asked. "Kissing should make you smile."

It made him confused.

"Kiss her again. Kiss her again." Justin slapped his knees in time to his chanting.

Kip wasn't even going to look his way because that meant looking at Nicole.

"Look, the next group is getting to run. Why don't we watch them? After all, that's what I bought the tickets for." He clasped his hands together, leaning forward and away from Nicole. He tried to focus on the riders, but he could smell her perfume, hear her talking quietly to Tristan. In his peripheral vision he saw her tuck her hair behind her ears, pull her jacket closer against the gathering chill of the evening.

Then the horn blew and he was drawn into the race.

They watched the races until the sun went down. When the last wagon crossed the finish line followed by the last of the outriders, Kip stood up. "Let's try to beat the crowd out of here," he said, wishing he felt as casual as he hoped he sounded.

Nicole got up and caught Tristan by the hand. Without a backward glance, she headed toward the exit.

"We didn't have a ride on the Ferris wheel like you promised," Justin said, trotting alongside him.

"I never promised you a ride," Kip contradicted him.

Tristan looked back, leaning past Nicole. "Yes, you did. You said that when we go to Stampede you would take us on the Ferris wheel."

He might have. He couldn't remember. But it was getting late, and he wanted to get back to the ranch and away from Nicole. She was spinning him around in circles.

His messy life had no space for a woman. Especially not a woman like Nicole who was leaving, and leaving with his boys, if she had her way.

"We need to get back to the ranch," he said firmly.

"But you promised," Tristan wailed.

"If Uncle Kip says we have to go back then that's what we have to do," Nicole said quietly, backing him up.

He wasn't surprised that she did. She probably didn't want a repeat performance of that kiss.

Thankfully, there was no more opportunity for conversation as they made their way down the noisy concrete stairwell to ground level.

When they stepped outside, the cool evening air had eased away the heat of the day. In the gathering dusk, the lights of the rides sparkled and beckoned in time to the raucous beat of rock music. People were laughing, screaming, having fun.

He paused by the midway, unable to ignore the longing look on his nephews' faces.

Justin, ever looking for the tiniest chink in his uncle's armor, homed in on Kip's hesitation. "Please Uncle Kip. We've never been on a Ferris wheel. Never."

Tristan added his pleas to his brother's. "Our dad always said he would take us and now he can't."

Kip sighed. They were really pulling out the heavy artillery by bringing up Scott. He couldn't help a glance Nicole's way, as if to get her take on the situation.

She gave him a quick smile. "If you don't mind, I don't mind. I'm not in any rush to bring the boys back."

Of course she wouldn't be. When they got to

the ranch she knew that would be the end of her visit with the boys.

"We can take another walk along the midway," Kip said.

"And we can find the Ferris wheel?" Justin asked.

Like a terrier with a toy, just like Scott used to be. "We'll just walk for now," he said.

The mixture of smells made him realize they hadn't had anything to eat since the hot dog when they first arrived. "Anyone for something to eat?"

"Can I have a pretzel?" Justin asked in a fakely innocent voice.

Kip shot him a warning look. Did the little guy know the only pretzel stand was clear across the fairgrounds?

"How about a piece of pizza?" Nicole suggested.

"Mini donuts," Tristan shouted, pulling away from Nicole. Kip was about to call him back when Nicole managed to grab his hand and pull him back.

"We stay together," she said sternly. "Don't take off like that again."

Tristan looked down, suitably chastened.

"I'd love some mini donuts," Kip said. "Nicole? You game?"

"Yeah. I'm game. I don't think I've ever had mini donuts."

"And the Ferris wheel?" Justin pressed. "Have you ever been on the Ferris wheel?"

"Actually, no," Nicole said.

"You've never been on a Ferris wheel? Don't they have fairs in Toronto?" Kip asked.

"I've never been on one. I'd like to try a ride."

"Yay. You're the best, Auntie Nicole," Justin shouted.

Kip shot her a frown and she gave him a look of mock consternation. "What? I've never been on a Ferris wheel."

"Never?"

"No. Never."

That seemed odd to him. "I guess I'm outnumbered," he said with a sigh of resignation.

"Obviously good at math too," she said with a flash of a smile.

"Never been my strong point. I did drop out of high school, after all." Kip wasn't sure where this playful Nicole was coming from, but he was willing to go along.

Kip ordered a bag of donuts, paid for them and handed them out. Nicole took one and then glanced up at him. "I think that was a very admirable thing to do."

"Buy donuts or become a dropout?" He added a grin so she would know he had no regrets.

"Make the sacrifice." She popped a donut in her mouth. "And I'm not talking about donuts."

"Well, it wasn't a huge sacrifice." Kip pulled a hanky out of his pocket and wiped the sugar off Justin's cheek.

"That you even say that tells me a lot about you," Nicole said with a bemused look on her face.

"Like what?" He caught Justin's hand again as they made their way through the crowd. The fairground took on a magical quality in the evening. The outside world faded away and it was him, Nicole and the boys surrounded by nameless people. The boys were too busy looking around to pay attention to what he and Nicole were discussing.

"It tells me how much you value family, and what you're willing to do to keep your family together." The lights of the Tilt-A-Whirl sent flashes of orange, red and blue across her face, making her eyes sparkle. "The boys are very blessed to have you in their lives. You've done an amazing job with them."

Kip was taken aback at her comment, but he couldn't look away from her. Her words were like a balm to his soul. A recognition that what he had done was, at times, worth all the frustration and all the uncertainty.

"Thank you," he said releasing a slow smile.

She returned it. "When I saw how excited you

were, when I heard you talking about the chuck wagons, I sensed that you missed it more than you let on."

Kip tried to push her comment aside with a shrug. "It had to end eventually."

"You've still got your horses, though. When I see what those teams can do, I'm trying to think of the hours of training you've put into them." She touched his shoulder, as if trying to convince him. "I can't imagine that you can stand to be away from that for long."

"I've got the boys," he said, gripping Justin's hand as they meandered through the crowds. "They're my responsibility. Like I said, I can't be leaving them alone every weekend." His words came out a bit harsher than he intended. He got the feeling that she was trying to make him wish he didn't have Tristan and Justin.

"Your mother can take care of the boys, and Isabelle can do more."

Kip was surprised by her reply. He was so sure she was going to tell him how much easier his life would be without the boys, which would bolster her case.

"Isabelle has had her own troubles," he said, defending his little sister.

"You lost a brother too."

Darkness entered Kip's soul. "Whatever happened to me is my own fault."

"How so?"

"Doesn't matter." He struggled to keep his emotions in check, flashes of that horrible day coming one after the other, the tangle of the reins, the horse struggling to pull free, Scott lying underneath.

"I understand from your mother that you blame yourself for what happened to Scott."

She spoke quietly, but her words laid his soul bare.

"Why do you care?"

"I've seen what guilt can do," she said, shooting him a quick glance. "And how it can distort a person's view of himself."

She hadn't answered his question, but he suspected she wouldn't. He thought of what she had told him the other night and wondered if she regretted telling him all she had.

"I understand it was your horse he was riding," she added.

Didn't look like she was quitting. With a sigh, he gave in. "Yeah. It was mine. A green-broke horse that Scott shouldn't have been riding."

Nicole nodded. "He chose to ride it, didn't he?"

Kip frowned. "You sound like my mother."

"That's not a bad thing." Nicole shot him a sideways glance, her mouth lifted in a faint smile. "Your mother is right."

Kip shrugged aside her comment. "You can

color it anyway you want, the reality is he'd still be here if he hadn't gotten on that horse."

"Could you have stopped him from getting on that horse, and would you have?"

Her quiet question set him back.

"He was an adult, and he made his own choices," Nicole continued. "I don't think you need to carry that responsibility. No one else seems to think you should."

Her softly spoken words rearranged thoughts and ideas he'd held for the past six months. Guilt he had carried since he pulled Scott out from underneath the horse.

Then, to his further surprise, he felt her hand on his arm. "You're a good man, Kip, and you're an even better brother. I don't know many men who would let their brother and two little boys move in with him when he already has a mother and a sister to take care of."

He glanced over at her, her soft smile easing into his soul. Then puzzlement took over. "Why are you telling me this? Aren't you supposed to be making me out to be the bad guy?" His eyes ticked over her face, then met her gaze.

She didn't look away. "You're not the bad guy."

Kip didn't reply, not sure what to make of her. Was she flirting with him?

"You just happen to be caught in a bad situation." Then she looked away.

What was she doing? Was she playing him?

He blew out his breath, not sure what to think. Then he glanced over at her. She was watching him again. That had been happening a lot lately, but this time as their eyes met, he felt a deeper, surprising emotion.

More than appeal. More than attraction. Her story the other night had shown him a glimpse into the inner workings of Nicole Williams. And yes, he felt sorry for her, but at the same time he'd been given something precious. He suspected that someone as private as she didn't share her history with too many people.

"Why are you guys talking about our dad?" Justin said, suddenly speaking up.

"We're just remembering things." Time to change the subject. "And you have sugar on your face." Kip brushed away the shiny granules clinging to his lip.

"So does Auntie Nicole," Justin said, pointing with one sugar-coated hand.

"So she does."

"Where?" Nicole asked, brushing at her face.

"There." Kip pointed it out to her with a smile.

Nicole wiped her cheek, then the other one. "No, I don't."

"It's right here." Kip brushed the sugar from her chin. Then his fingers slowed; lingered an extra second.

She swallowed and her free hand caught his, her delicate fingers encircling his wrist. "Thanks," she whispered, her smile settling into his soul.

"You're welcome."

"Hey, there's the Ferris wheel." Justin pulled on Kip's hand, breaking the moment. "Let's go for a ride."

"Here goes," Kip said, letting Justin pull him along.

The Ferris wheel towered above them, buckets swinging and people laughing.

"I'll get in line, you get the tickets," Nicole suggested. She pulled out her wallet, but Kip waved it off.

"My treat," he said.

"Thank you." She gave him another smile and Kip almost started whistling as he walked to the ticket booth. But he didn't. Justin was looking up at him as if trying to figure out why his uncle Kip was in such a good mood.

It was just a fun evening, he told himself as he paid for the tickets. Just a casual time with an attractive woman and his nephews. Their nephews, he corrected.

When he returned, the line behind them had grown. When they got to the front, Kip saw that the seats held four people. He had assumed that he would go on one seat with Justin and Nicole and Tristan on another. From the looks of the line, he doubted each would be allowed to have their own seat.

"Move along, go sit down," the operator called out. "Four to a seat, please."

"I want to sit on the outside," Tristan said, scurrying to the far side of the bench.

"Me too." Justin added, dropping into the other side.

Which left the middle for Kip and Nicole.

Kip didn't look at Nicole as they sat down. The operator lowered the bar, they were secured in, and the wheel moved ahead to let the next group of four on.

"We're going to be real high," Tristan said, his voice full of awe. "It's like we're in another world."

Kip sat back. Nicole did the same, just as the wheel jerked forward pushing them against each other.

"Sorry," Kip said, trying to give her some space.

"Uncle Kip, you're hogging my space," Justin said.

There was no getting around it. He and Nicole were spending the next few minutes sitting close together. He looked over at her to gauge her reaction only to find her grinning at him.

"I guess we're stuck together," she said.

Kip grinned back. "I guess." He didn't look away, his mind flicking back to the kiss he had given her. He thought of her hand, encircling his wrist.

Then, before he could change his mind, he slipped his arm around her shoulders. "May as well get comfortable," he said, and she didn't pull away.

The wheel turned slowly around, each movement bringing them closer to the top. When it stopped there, the boys were speechless. Their seat swung a bit, suspended above the fairgrounds, removed from the noise and music. Like Tristan had said, it was as if they were in another world.

Nicole shivered, and Kip capitalized on that and pulled her closer. Her face, framed by her golden hair, was a pale silhouette against a starry sky.

Everything slipped away and it was as if they were the only two people in this endless space.

He leaned closer and she met him partway. Then he kissed her. Gently. Slowly.

He pulled away, a gentle sigh easing out of him. She didn't look away. Neither did he. Their silence extended the moment. Then, with a jerk, the Ferris wheel moved along one more time.

Kip kept his arm around her and she reached up and caught his hand, as if anchoring him to her.

"Wow, this is so awesome," Justin said, still looking over the edge.

"I love this," Tristan replied from his seat.

"I know what they mean," Kip murmured.

Though Nicole looked away from him, she tightened her grip on his hand.

The wheel was full and then they were moving steadily and with each revolution, at the top, Kip looked at Nicole and she looked at him. They didn't repeat the kiss, but each time their eyes met it was as if they had.

And each time their eyes met Kip's heart beat a little harder and his optimism burned a little brighter.

Could he and Nicole have a future?

Did he dare think that far?

Chapter Twelve

"Here's your cowboy hat." Kip took the white straw hat he had bought from the kiosk and dropped it on Nicole's head. He lifted her chin with his knuckle, his rough skin rasping on hers. "There you go, Nicole Williams. Now you're an Alberta cowgirl."

"That sounds official." Nicole pushed the hat further on her head, wishing her heart didn't jump at his every touch.

"Auntie Nicole is a cowgirl." Tristan jumped up and down.

"Now she has to go riding horses," Justin said hopefully.

Nicole didn't say anything to bolster his cause. She'd said quite enough to Kip already. And she had let Kip Cosgrove do quite enough, kissing her on the Ferris wheel.

She tried to remind herself that Kip wasn't her friend.

She had discovered in the past few days, however, that he wasn't her enemy either. He was simply a man doing what he was asked to do. A man living up to his responsibilities.

But the memory of that kiss and the utterly spontaneous one earlier lingered both in her mind and on her lips.

"We're not talking about the horses now," Kip said with a note of finality. "We're going home. It's way past your bedtime."

The boys were obviously tired because they didn't even argue as they trudged back to the truck. They got in and settled down for the long ride back.

Nicole tried not to look at Kip as he drove, his face illuminated by the glow of the dashboard lights. She tried to push the kiss to the back of her mind as she pulled herself back into reality mode.

She took her hat off and held it on her lap, as if easing away from the day—turning back into Nicole, the girl who wore business suits and high heels and attended business meetings. Not a cowgirl in blue jeans who let a man kiss her on the Ferris wheel.

"I was wondering if we could discuss my visit tomorrow," Nicole said quietly after they reached the city limits. "I have a conference call in the late afternoon. Would it be possible to come in the morning?"

"You can't," Justin piped up from the backseat of the truck. "We go to church on Sunday."

"Of course." Nicole tapped her fingers on her arm, thinking. They'd gone last week while she was at the motel sending out flurries of emails about work.

"Why don't you come to church with us?" Justin asked. "Then you can sit with us."

"I'm not so sure—"

"Please come," Tristan added. "It's kind of long sometimes, but then we can see you in the morning too."

Nicole's resistance softened as she looked back at the boys, considering the invitation.

"You're welcome to come," Kip said quietly.

The last time Nicole had been in church was for her mother's funeral. That service had been full of sorrow, regret and a heavy layer of guilt.

Though attending church would mean she'd see the boys, it would also mean seeing Kip.

That's a dangerous place to go, she reminded herself. This evening was supposed to be a blip on your radar. An experience—a date—that she could put away in the memory chest.

"I'd like it if you could come," Kip added, his voice quiet.

His comment, combined with his tender smile, swept away her resistance. "What time does the service start?"

"Ten o'clock."

"I'll see how my morning goes," she said cautiously.

It was just church, she reminded herself as she sat back in the truck. Going back to church could be a good thing.

"I'm bored," Justin said from the backseat. "And I don't want to play I Spy again."

Nicole twisted in her seat. "Do you guys know any songs? Maybe you could sing them for me."

"I don't like to sing," Tristan said.

"I'm really bored," Justin repeated.

Nicole pulled out her phone. "If you guys can share, I can show you a game that you can play on my phone."

Their eyes grew to four large circles of surprise. "Really?"

"Cool." Justin had his hand out for her phone.

"You can't have it, I want it."

Nicole hesitated looking from Justin to Tristan.

"You started something now," Kip said. She could hear the smile in his voice.

"You'll have to take turns," she said. She turned on a timer function, started up the game and handed it to Tristan. "When this bell dings, then it's Justin's turn."

"How come he gets to go first?" Justin whined.

"Because we love him more," Kip said.

Nicole shot him look of shock. What was he doing? What was he saying? She was about to reprimand him when she heard Justin's giggle.

"No, you don't, Uncle Kip," he said, completely unperturbed by the comment.

"Oh, yes, I do," Kip said, glancing in his rearview mirror at his nephew.

"You love us both the same," Tristan chimed in, quickly figuring out how to play the game.

Nicole tried to absorb what had happened. The boys were so utterly confident of their uncle's love that his outrageous statement was greeted with humor.

Did those boys have any idea of how blessed they were, Nicole thought, her heart contracting with envy?

"Oops. I think I pushed the wrong button…hey, is this your house?" Justin held out the phone to Nicole. Somehow he had gotten into her picture file.

"Yes, that's where I live. Here, let me find that game for you again."

"Uncle Kip, look at Auntie Nicole's house." Justin held the phone toward Kip who dutifully glanced at it.

"Very nice. Very impressive," he said in a tone that implied anything but.

"Do you have any other pictures?" Justin asked.

Nicole thought of the one photo she had of her father on her phone but felt a surprising reluctance to show them. Some of that had to do with the man sitting across the truck from her, frowning now. The other part was a reluctance to bring that part of her life into this moment.

"I'll get you the game again," she said, taking the phone and getting them back on track.

The boys took a couple of turns with her phone, their chatter slowly fading away. Half an hour later the phone lay between them and the only sound in the truck was their deep, rhythmic breathing. Nicole glanced into the vehicles passing them, the stores beyond the traffic—everywhere but at the man driving the truck.

The man who had kissed her twice.

She'd been kissed before. It was nothing new. She'd be kissed again. Someday by the man she would marry.

Which wouldn't happen anytime soon, she reasoned. Not when she had so much happening. The boys. Her father. Her job.

"I want to thank you," Kip said, his deep voice breaking into her thoughts and pulling her attention back to him.

"For what?"

Kip was looking ahead at the flow of traffic, his face illuminated by the glow of the streetlights.

"For what you said about Scott and about guilt." He turned his head, his eyes catching her gaze. "I guessed you know a bit about that too."

Nicole sighed. "I do, or rather, I did." What happened between her and Tricia was in the past.

"I'm guessing you're talking about your sister."

Nicole nodded.

"How did you two get along?" he asked, gently prying.

Nicole shrugged. "Tricia and I got along really great when she was a little girl."

"And later?

"That's when we started fighting."

"About the usual girl stuff?"

She wished. "No. It was bigger than lipstick and borrowed blue jeans."

"I'm guessing she was a rebellious person."

Nicole shifted down into her seat, her eyes following the road. Against her will, scenes from the last time she saw her sister edged into her mind. The angry words she'd said. The accusations. Things she should never have said. "We had a nasty fight, and the next morning she was gone. I never heard anything from her after that."

"She didn't write your parents either. That must have been hard for them."

"It was. My mother cried every night for months after Tricia left."

"And your father?"

"It was especially hard for him. Tricia was his daughter and she was gone."

"You make it sound like she was his *only* daughter."

"I know she wasn't…" Nicole shifted in her seat, wishing he would stop this line of questioning. "But I was his adopted daughter. Tricia was his natural child. Of course it would hurt that she chose to leave."

"What are you trying to say?" Kip sounded like he really wanted to hear what she had to say.

Nicole paused, searching for the right words to formulate her thoughts. "I was eight years old when Sam and Norah adopted me. I know it's hard to bond with children that aren't yours. I experienced that with my aunt and in most of the foster homes I stayed in. That's the reality. Tricia was Sam and Norah's biological child. Of course it would hurt my father more when she left."

"What…why would you say that?"

Tricia was surprised at the thread of anger in his voice. "Like I said, it's reality, Kip. If you found out that the boys…" she paused as she shot a quick glance over her shoulder. Thankfully both Justin and Tristan were still fast asleep, heads at awkward angles, mouths slightly open. Utterly innocent and utterly adorable. She cleared her throat and tried again. "If you found out that the boys weren't Scott's—" and he would, she thought "—weren't your nephews, wouldn't that make a difference for you?"

"What? Are you kidding?" Kip sounded incredulous. As if he couldn't believe she would even speak those words aloud.

"No. I'm not."

Kip leaned forward, a deep frown furrowing his brow. "I love the boys. They were always as much mine as Scott's, even though they were his boys." He thumbed his hat back on his head and shot her a frown. "They're woven into my heart. They're a part of me that I can't imagine living without. That's not because of biology. It's because I made a choice to take care of them and to take them in, and weaved through that choice came love."

Nicole's heart stuttered at the sincerity in his voice. At the intensity of his gaze.

"Even if I found out they weren't Scott's boys that wouldn't affect how much I love them. That wouldn't change anything." He sighed and turned his attention back to the road. "I love them. With all my heart."

Tears pricked her eyes at the sincerity in his voice. Each word he spoke dove into her heart and attached itself, creating another connection to this man. A connection that she had yearned, since she was a little girl, to have with her own father.

"I don't want to turn everything into a battle over the boys," Kip added, his voice growing quiet. "You know where I stand on that matter." He sighed. "You need to know that these boys are a part of me that I can't live without."

He looked at her again and she held his gaze a moment. She gave into an impulse and covered his hand with hers. "I know that." She gave his hand a light squeeze, then drew away before he could see the tears threatening in her eyes.

She blinked, reasoning the moment of sadness away. She had always accepted that as the adopted daughter, she wouldn't have the same connection to Sam as Tricia had.

However, in spite of her practical reasoning, the lonely-little-girl part of her wished that for even a moment, she could have heard Sam say about her what Kip had said about his nephews. That she could have received even a particle of the affection Kip lavished so freely on children that weren't his.

As Nicole stared out the window, her thoughts drifted back to her father. To the moment she had with him before she left for Alberta.

He had clung to her hand with a strength she had never felt before, the frustration with the illness that kept him in bed burning in his eyes. He would settle for nothing less than the boys' coming to Toronto and he would do what he could on his end to ensure that happened. At the time she'd taken on the cause, feeling it was another opportunity to atone. To earn his love.

And now?

Nicole wasn't so sure of the rightness of their claim anymore.

You know what it's like to be uprooted.

But she also knew what it was like to yearn for a place where she belonged, body and soul. A place where she was a blood relative. Because no matter what Kip might say, she knew from personal experience that blood truly was thicker than water.

Tricia had been blood. Nicole had been water.

Nicole's mind drifted back and forth, her thoughts wearing on her as she slowly spun down into a half sleep. Her mind drifted from thoughts about her father into vague thoughts of Ferris wheels and Kip's kiss…that wonderful kiss…

"Hey. Nicole. We're here." Kip's voice came from far away and Nicole blinked, trying to orient herself. Her mouth felt dry and her eyes full of sand. She blinked as she looked up at Kip's face as he stood in the open door of the truck.

He touched her cheek and with her dreams still clouding her mind, Nicole caught his hand. His eyes were softly lit by the half moon above and she couldn't look away.

"You were sleeping," he whispered, his hand cupping her cheek.

"I'm sorry," she mumbled, struggling to pull her thoughts back to reality. She shivered as the cool night sifted over her. Then she looked up at him and smiled. "Thanks for a fun evening."

Kip's fingers caressed her cheek. "I enjoyed it. A lot."

She should look away and end this connection, but the moment seemed surreal. Ethereal. Then, with the kiss he had given her on the Ferris wheel still vivid in her mind, and with her soul yearning for the closeness she'd experienced, she leaned forward and brushed her lips over his.

Kip whispered her name, then drew her into his arms and they kissed again. A kiss born of longing and connection. A kiss that anchored them in a way that nothing else had.

A kiss that rocked Nicole's world.

She pulled away, her heart thrumming in her chest. What was she doing? This was dangerous. And confusing. And…

Wonderful.

Kissing Kip was like coming home.

Chapter Thirteen

Nicole smoothed her hair, checked her lipstick in the rearview mirror of her car and took in a deep breath.

It's just a gathering of people, she reminded herself, pushing aside memories of a God she used to think cared about her. You're only here so you can see your nephews.

She slung her leather purse over her shoulder and strode across the parking lot to the white stucco church, her high heels clicking on the asphalt. The summer sun warmed her shoulders, and for a moment she regretted the suit and silk shirt she had chosen for today.

When she had gone to church with the Williams family, Norah had insisted on wearing their best clothes. A sign of respect and consideration she had said, as Tricia fought putting on the cute dress that always matched Nicole's. Only Nicole was allowed to brush Tricia's dark hair and tie it up in a ribbon, and once they were all ready, only Nicole was allowed to help Tricia put her coat on.

Nicole's steps faltered as the old memories surfaced. On the heels of that came the reminder of her beloved sister's last wishes.

That the boys be with their father and with her.

A young father and mother and their two children came out of a car ahead of her, and as they got out, the woman smiled at Nicole and wished her a good morning.

Another elderly couple did the same as she neared the church building.

Friendly, Nicole thought, as she pushed open one of the large glass doors of the building. The buzz of conversation greeted her. People young and old milled about the entrance, chatting and visiting with one another. She held back for a moment, assessing and looking around. People knew each other. She didn't belong.

She pushed the thought aside as she worked her way through the gathering to the double doors she saw past the people. Once she got to the main auditorium, things were a little quieter, but not much. People were settling into pews, still talking amongst one another.

The front stage area held a lectern, a set of

drums, a piano and a few guitars standing upright on stands.

"Welcome to our church," a young man said, handing her a piece of paper. "I hope you like the service."

Nicole glanced at his blue jeans topped with a T-shirt and open shirt and felt overdressed.

"You visiting here?" he asked.

"Yes, I am." She looked over the people already seated, that out-of-place feeling returning. She didn't know anyone. "Is the Cosgrove family here yet?"

"They're sitting where they always sit." Nicole looked in the direction he was pointing and immediately recognized Kip's tall figure and his broad shoulders. Justin and Tristan sat on either side of him.

Kip's mother sat in her wheelchair in the aisle beside him, which made Nicole frown. Why wasn't she using her walker?

She brushed the questions aside and with a nod to the young man strode down the aisle. She came at the pew from the other side and slid into the empty spot beside Justin.

Kip, who had been talking to his mother while Nicole sat down, turned suddenly. As their eyes met, Nicole felt that sudden jolt of awareness that not only surprised her but disconcerted her.

·· In spite of her mental warnings, she let her smile linger and shift.

Kip's returning smile softened his features and created another, more peculiar tingle.

"Auntie Nicole, you came." Justin grinned, tucking his warm, slightly damp hand inside hers.

"I want to sit by Auntie Nicole too," Tristan whined.

"Okay, go ahead, but be quiet," Kip warned.

Tristan scooted past Justin and sat triumphantly on her other side.

"You guys look really spiffy," she said, glancing from one to the other. She hardly recognized the shining faces, the slicked-back hair and the white shirts and dark pants she remembered ironing the other day.

Justin made a face. "Gramma always makes us dress up for church. Says it's a sign of respect."

Nicole felt a touch of melancholy at the words, so similar to what she'd just been thinking. Her mother used to say the same thing whenever they went to church and Tricia would argue about what to wear.

Mary leaned forward and waved to Nicole. "Hey, Nicole. Good to see you here. I didn't think you'd come."

Nicole hadn't thought she would either, but here she was. She returned Mary's smile, but as she sat back, her eyes naturally drifted to Kip, who was still watching her. His expression had grown serious, his eyebrows pulled together in a frown of, what? Concentration? Disapproval?

Nicole turned her attention back to boys, trying to keep their high spirits reasonably under control. This was church, after all.

"We told Gramma about the Stampede," Justin said. "And the midway and the Ferris wheel." Nicole's heart jolted at that. Had the boys seen their kiss? "She said it sounded like fun."

"Can I play with your phone again?" Justin asked.

"It's my turn. You played with it last time," Tristan said.

Nicole shook her head. "It's not respectful," she said, building on what Mary had already told them.

They looked like they were about to argue when a figure dropped into the pew beside Justin.

Isabelle.

She wore a skirt today, short and snug, and under that leggings with lace at the bottom and ballet flats with bright orange flowers. Her shirt was a riot of pink and purple overtop of an orange tank top. A white scarf was draped around her neck.

Obviously still trying to find a personal style.

Isabelle shot Nicole a frown. "What are you doing here?"

"And a good morning to you," Nicole said with a bright smile, determined not to let Isabelle push her around.

"Auntie Nicole, when can we talk to our Grandpa on the phone again?"

Nicole shot a frown their way. "What Grandpa are you talking about?"

"The one in Toronto, silly," Justin shot back.

"You don't have a Grandpa in Toronto." Isabelle spoke the words with smug authority.

"Yes, we do," Tristan said. "Auntie Nicole let us talk to him."

"Why are you telling them that?" Isabelle gave Nicole a look that was supposed to be disdainful, but in her eyes, Nicole caught a hint of fear. "My Dad was their only Grandpa."

Though she treated the boys like they were nothing but a nuisance, Nicole sensed Isabelle would be just as upset as her mother was if the boys were to leave.

Nicole looked away, the moment of vulnerability creating an unease.

Things were getting complicated, she thought, her eyes drifting over to Kip and beyond that to Mary. Complicated and confusing. She wasn't as sure of what she needed to do as when she first came here. She wasn't so sure she wanted to take the boys away from this home.

Or Kip.

She brushed the second thoughts aside. She was letting her emotions interfere with what she knew was right. Tricia had wanted her parents to take care of her boys. What Nicole thought of the situation had nothing to do with that.

The music started up and everyone stood. The leader announced the song they were going to sing and words flashed up on a screen in the front of the church.

The song had a catchy tune and soon she was singing along, surprised to find herself enjoying the music. The song segued into another, quieter song.

The words to this song were familiar to her. It was an older hymn, and the combination of music drew up pictures of Tricia and her parents standing in church together. The memories created an unwelcome thickness in her throat

She stopped singing, pulling back from the emotions and the memories. By the time she had everything under control the song, thankfully, was ended.

They were greeted by a minister who welcomed them all and led them in prayer, followed by another song.

As they went through the service, Nicole's self-control returned. Besides, she was distracted enough keeping the boys from fidgeting too much or talking too loudly.

"You boys have to be a little quieter," she whispered as they sat down after another song.

Justin sighed. "Uncle Kip always says that too."

"Uncle Kip is right," Nicole said, slipping her arms around the boys' shoulders as the minister encouraged them to turn to 1 Corinthians 13.

Tristan pulled a Bible from the pew ahead of him, laying it on Nicole's lap and gesturing for her to look it up.

She felt a moment's panic as she opened it and flipped through the pages. The name of the book was familiar and she remembered that it was in the New Testament, but that was it. The minister started reading, but she still hadn't found the passage.

"Don't you know where it is, Auntie Nicole?" Tristan asked.

"No. Sorry." Flip, flip. Still no luck. She knew the book, not where it was located.

Then Kip leaned past Justin and turned to the right spot.

Nicole's cheeks burned and for a moment she felt like she didn't belong here. Couldn't even find a book of the Bible.

Her eyes flew over the page trying to catch up to the minister. There it was.

"...If I give all I possess to the poor and surrender my body to the flames, but have not love, I gain nothing.

Love is patient, love is kind. It does not envy, it does not boast, it is not proud. It is not rude, it is not self-seeking, it is not easily angered, it keeps no record of wrongs." The words came at her in a steady rhythm. Her mind slipped back to her father and how she'd yearned every day for not only his respect, but even more, his love.

"….Love does not delight in evil, but rejoices with the truth. It always protects, always trusts, always hopes, always perseveres." A haunting tune wove itself through the words as he read. The tune was from a song she remembered Norah Williams singing when she was a young girl. It was a song about how deep the Father's love, how vast beyond all measure. The song had spoken to her then, had called to the part of her that had longed for her biological father's love, then, later, tried to earn Sam's love. Then Tricia left and the song and the feelings they evoked were buried in the barrage of pain and sorrow that followed.

"…And now these three remain. Faith, hope and love, but the greatest of these is love."

The sorrows of the past beat at her, yet, in spite of that, below the turmoil, the words of the passage offered something more.

The love of God. The steadfast and faithful love of God.

Then the minister closed the Bible, leaned on the podium and started speaking.

"This passage is not simply about love. To put it in context, the people of Corinth wanted one thing—certain spiritual gifts—but needed something even more important. Love. Love is just a small word," he continued. "A word that has been thrown about so often, we've sucked all the power out of it. Love is a word that the Creator of the world not only invented, but embodies."

His words drew Nicole on as he spoke of God's faithful love and how it satisfies all our needs. How love is such a small word for the powerful thing God had done when He gave up His own life for the sake of sinful beings.

"Who would put the needs of someone else before such imperfect beings? Only God has that kind of love. The love our parents have is powerful, but not as powerful as God's love for us. This love comes to us as a gift. Freely given. We don't deserve it and we can't earn it."

Nicole listened to the pastor, seeking the hope and love he claimed was hers for the taking, just as Kip had told her the other night. A love that didn't need to be earned because it could never be earned. Love that was freely given, in spite of the cost, and meant to be freely received.

The words slipped into the empty spaces in Nicole's heart. It seemed she had spent all of her time at the Williamses' home feeling as if she had to earn their love. Her father reinforced that feeling with each expectation he had of her—work at his side in the foundation, live at home and now make sure that Tricia's boys come to where he thought they should be.

What else could she do? It was her reality.

Then, it seemed too soon, the service was over. They stood for the final song, and as the notes rang away, Tristan tugged on her hand.

"It's time to go," he said, dragging her out of her circling thoughts.

They were stopped at the end of the pew by the flow of people all exiting at once. As Nicole was drawn back into reality, she pulled Tristan back as he tried to wiggle his way through the crowd. "Why are you in such a rush?" he asked.

"We have to get to Auntie Doreen's right away," Tristan said. "So we can get the best toys."

"Auntie Doreen's? What are you talking about?"

"We always go to Auntie Doreen's for lunch," Justin said, in a tone that implied she should know this.

Nicole glanced back over her shoulder, but Kip was exiting the other aisle, pushing his mother's wheelchair. She'd have to wait until he caught up to her to find out what was going on.

The boys had their own plan. They pulled her

along, and as they exited the auditorium, someone called the boys' names.

"Oh, brother," Justin said, throwing his hands up in an dramatic gesture. "Now we're going to be late." But he stopped and turned around.

A young woman carrying a tiny baby in one arm and leading a little girl roughly the same age as the boys walked up to them. "Hey, guys. There you are," she said to them.

The woman's hair was the same shade as Kip's and her eyes the same color. Her features were closer to Isabelle's than her brother's. When she smiled at the boys, Nicole could see Mary Cosgrove in the shape of her mouth.

"I'm guessing you're Nicole," the woman said. When she met Nicole's eyes, her smile tightened, as if she had to force it.

Nicole wasn't surprised. She didn't think Kip's sister would be thrilled to meet the woman who was laying a claim to her nephews.

Alleged nephews, she reminded herself.

"Hello, I'm Doreen. Kip's sister." Doreen raised her chin by way of greeting, her hands otherwise occupied with two of her children. "Would you like to join us for lunch?"

Doreen knew who she was and what she hoped to do, yet she was asking her over?

She was about to give the very polite young

mother an easy out when Justin blurted out, "You have to come, Auntie Nicole. You have to."

"Please, come. Please," Tristan added, pulling on her hand as if he hoped to physically drag a response from her. "We can ride with you and tell you where to go so you don't get lost."

"I don't know—" she hesitated. If she didn't go along, this time in church would be her only time with the boys.

"Come and join us," Doreen added. "Kip asked me to ask you, but it would be our pleasure if you came." Her smile held a bit more warmth, and Nicole relented.

"I'd be glad to." Truth was, the thought of returning to the stark and plain motel room held little appeal. It reminded her too much of the times her aunt would bring her to her father when he was working near the town.

It had nothing to do with the fact that Kip had asked Doreen to invite her. Nothing at all.

Fifteen minutes and some rather convoluted directions later, Nicole was parking her car beside an older house on an acreage outside of Millarville. Trucks and ride-on toys dotted the lawn. Flowers spilled out of pots hanging from brackets on the side of the house and set up against a crooked concrete step. Shrub-filled flower beds nestled up against the wooden siding of the older home. The entire place looked homey and comfortable and welcoming.

"Let's go, Auntie Nicole," the boys called out as they ran up the walk.

As she got out, Kip pulled up his truck beside her. Mary Cosgrove sat in the front seat.

"You go inside," she told the boys. "I'll help Uncle Kip."

The boys didn't even look back as they raced over the lawn to the house.

"Where's Isabelle?" Nicole asked as Kip got out of the truck.

"She rode with Doreen." Kip pulled a wheelchair out of the back of the truck.

Nicole frowned. "Where's your mom's walker?"

"She said her knee was really bothering her," Kip said as he snapped open the chair. "So she's taking a break."

"She'll never heal from the surgery properly if she doesn't keep working her legs."

Kip gave her an odd look as he wheeled the chair to the door of the truck, and she wasn't sure what to make of it. Then he held her gaze and smiled a slow-release smile. She wasn't sure what to make of that either.

"Why don't you tell her that?" he said quietly.

"I will." Nicole waited until Kip opened the door of the truck, then watched as Mary worked her way into the chair.

"So you found your way here," Mary said with a grunt as she settled into the chair. "I thought for sure those boys would try to take you through the shortcut and get lost."

"We made it okay. Why aren't you using your walker?"

"My knee has been bothering me," Mary said with a quick glance back at Kip as if hoping he would intervene.

"If you don't keep moving, then all the pain from the surgery will be for nothing and you'll be back to where you started before your surgery."

"Well, I suppose." Mary bit her lip, as if thinking. "But I don't have my walker now."

"Kip and I can help you to the house. You can lean on our arms, and then you can sit on a normal chair and not look like such an invalid."

"I guess so," Mary said with a heavy sigh. She looked up at Nicole with narrow eyes. "You're a bit bossy, you know."

"So I've been told." Nicole caught Kip's gaze and tried not to roll her eyes. Kip grinned.

They walked slowly up to the house just as Isabelle came to the door. She glared at Nicole, then back at her mother.

"Wow, Mom. You're not using the wheelchair," she said with an admiring tone.

"Nicole told me I could do it, and I guess I can."

Isabelle shot Nicole a frown, but then reached out for her mother's arm. "I'll take over from here."

Nicole relinquished her hold as Isabelle ushered Mary into the house.

Kip blew out his breath and shot her a quick smile. "Thanks for the help. For some reason she won't listen to me."

"You have to be firm."

"You sound like a mother," Kip's smile widened.

"I used to boss Tricia around something awful." Nicole felt a momentary pang at the memory. "I guess I'm a natural."

"You are that." Kip touched her face, his fingers lingering on her cheek.

Nicole's heart stuttered in her chest and, cheeks burning, she stepped into the house.

Mary was already settled in a chair, looking quite satisfied with herself, a cup of tea beside her on a TV tray. Isabelle was lying on the couch, reading a magazine.

"Hey, Kip, you made it." Doreen called out as she came into the living room, carrying her baby. She reached up to give Kip a one-armed hug that he reached down to return. Then he bent over the baby curled up in his sister's arm and touched its tiny head with one finger. "Hey, little one," he said quietly. "How are you?"

Nicole swallowed at the sight of this big, tough cowboy bent over this little baby, a look of tenderness on his face.

Doreen glanced over at Nicole. "I hope this isn't too overwhelming. Kip told me that you're used to a little more sedate lifestyle."

Nicole wondered what else Kip had told his sister.

"I'll be fine. I like kids."

Doreen's gaze flashed from Nicole to Kip. "That's good." She jostled the now-fussing baby.

"What's her name?" Nicole asked.

"Emily."

Nicole gave into an impulse and held her arms out. "Can I hold her?"

Doreen's frown was fleeting, but then she nodded. "That'd be great."

She handed the little bundle over with all the confidence of an experienced mother. Nicole felt a little awkward as the baby squawked a protest, but when Emily settled in Nicole's arms, her tiny mouth stretched open in a yawn. Her delicate fingers stretched and with a sigh as gentle as a cobweb, she drifted back to sleep.

"She's so beautiful," Nicole whispered, stroking her petal-soft cheek with one finger.

"I think we'll keep her around for a while. At least until the terrible twos. Might have to see if we can farm her out then—" Then Doreen sucked in a quick breath. "I'm sorry…I didn't mean…that was thoughtless."

"Why don't I help you and Ron get lunch on the table," Kip said, taking his sister's arm. "Just make yourself at home," he said to Nicole.

Nicole presumed that Kip wanted to have a "chat" with his sister. She also presumed that he had told her about her past, which surprised her.

"Come sit over here," Mary said, brushing a stuffed duck and a book off the chair beside her. "Don't worry about Doreen. She tends to talk before she thinks. The hazards of being a mother."

"That's okay. It didn't bother me." Nicole just smiled as she slowly lowered herself into the chair. Little Emily pursed her lips and rolled her head, then settled again. Nicole touched her face again, then let the baby curl her tiny fingers around hers. "Look how delicate her fingernails are. Like little grains of rice," she remarked, taking in the wonder of this brand-new person.

"Pretty amazing," Mary said quietly. "It never gets old."

"Did you want to hold her?" Nicole asked, realizing that she was taking this baby away from her own grandmother.

Mary waved away her offer. "I get to see her enough."

Nicole was secretly glad. She didn't want to

relinquish her precious burden. It had been years and years since she'd seen a baby, much less held one.

As she looked down at Emily, she wondered about her biological mother's love. Wondered how she had felt when she held her. Wondered how Tricia felt when the twins were born.

Her heart contracted at the thought.

She heard lowered voices coming from the kitchen and she presumed Kip and his sister were talking. About her plans? About the boys?

"Don't worry," Mary said quietly. "He'll be back."

A flush worked its way up Nicole's neck. "I was just...it's not..."

Mary patted her on the shoulder. "He's a good man, my Kip. Please remember that," she said, lowering her voice.

Nicole caught Mary's gaze. Did she know what was building between Nicole and her son? "I know he is a good man," she said, her voice full of conviction.

Isabelle glared at her over the top of her magazine. "Then why are you taking the boys—" Isabelle stopped herself, threw her magazine down on the couch and got up. "I'm going outside."

But as she left, Nicole caught a glimmer in her eyes. She suspected the glimmer came from unshed tears and the sight tangled her emotions even more.

The longer she stayed here and the more she got to know the Cosgrove family, the more confused she became about what she had come to do. She wondered if, when the time came, she could do it?

Chapter Fourteen

"So the boys tell me you went to the chuck-wagon races yesterday, Kip," Alex said, reaching across the dining room table for another bun. "That must have been interesting."

If he only knew, Kip thought, slicing up a bun for Tristan and avoiding Nicole's gaze.

The entire family was grouped around the dining room table, kids interspersed between the adults, and conversations zipped back and forth and through each other.

"Yeah. Mike won his heat."

"Uncle Kip was so excited that he kissed Auntie Nicole," Justin piped up.

Kip wanted to elbow the little guy, but that would only draw even more attention to the situation.

"Do you miss it?" Alex asked, feeding another spoonful of soup to his youngest daughter, tactfully ignoring Justin's little outburst.

"What? You kissed Auntie Nicole?" Jenna, one of Doreen's older children, called across the table.

"Yeah. I missed racing the chucks." Kip ignored Jenna and tried not to catch Nicole's reaction to both the comment and his niece's reference to her as "Auntie Nicole." She sat across from him, and it was hard not to look over her way from time to time only to catch her looking at him.

"You beat Mike a bunch of times, didn't you?" Mary said. "Paul, don't blow your nose in the napkin, honey."

"I tied with him once at the Ponoka Stampede and I think I beat him at a race in Lethbridge." Kip stood up and helped himself to another bowl of soup from the huge pot in the middle of the table, then served up for two of Doreen's children as well.

As he did, he thought of the pictures of Nicole's home that the boys had found on Nicole's phone and so generously shown to him. The photos were small, but it wasn't hard to see the size of the house and the grounds surrounding it.

He doubted Nicole had ever had soup served to her out of an industrial sized pot plopped unceremoniously on an old wooden table, scarred from the doodlings of seven children.

He doubted she ever ate with a group of kids so noisy and rambunctious that half of the conversation consisted of reprimands and reminders to eat.

"I think you should do it again," Kristen, Doreen's second oldest daughter, said. "I loved watching you race."

"Uncle Kip takes us every year, at Christmas, on a sleigh ride," Jenna said to Nicole. "But he didn't this year."

Kip wished they could move to the usual topics of conversation. The weather, the kids, the crops, the kids, the neighbors, the kids.

"Have you ever ridden, Nicole?" Doreen said, wiping the face of a little child beside her while she spoke.

"Quite extensively. My parents owned a number of horses that my sister and I rode, though I spent more time with them than Tricia did. We were fortunate enough to have a barn that we could ride in on all year round."

Some barn, Kip thought, remembering the pictures of the arena and painted wooden fences. That barn looked in better shape than their house.

"You really should take Nicole out on the horses," Doreen said. "Or at least take her out in the wagon."

"I don't think I have time."

"You always had time before," his mother said.

Kip wasn't going to point out the obvious. That "before" was before Scott died. Before he didn't trust other people around his horses anymore.

Scott made his own choices. Nicole's comment echoed in his head at the same time as she focused her gaze on him.

"Wouldn't you love to go on a wagon ride with Kip's horses?" Doreen asked Nicole, pushing the point.

"Doreen…" Kip warned.

"I think it would be a wonderful to do something so idyllic." Nicole spoke quietly, but her subtext was clear as was her choice of words.

Idyllic indeed.

Doreen clapped her hands like a little kid. "Why don't you take Nicole out and then, tomorrow after school, I'll drop by with the kids and you can take them on a ride too? To make up for them not being able to go on their sleigh ride at Christmas."

Kip shot his sister an exasperated look, but she stared him down, looking as innocent as her little baby.

"I think it's a great idea and I'd love to go," Nicole said, adding one more layer of pressure.

Though he had other work waiting for him, Kip knew what he'd be doing tomorrow.

Unbidden, his gaze slipped to Nicole, only to catch her looking at him. For a moment he couldn't look away. For a moment, it was as if he'd lost himself in her eyes.

And that was a dangerous place to be.

* * *

"Are you sure you're okay with this?" Nicole glanced over at Kip as they walked to the corrals. She didn't want him to feel pressured, but at the same time the thought of going out on the wagon with him created a little thrum of excitement.

Kip sighed. "When my sister starts bossing me around, I just pull my hat lower, and smile and nod."

"Seems to be your default position around the women in your life."

Kip laughed. "That and keep a low profile."

Tristan and Justin were back at the house with Mary and Isabelle. To Nicole's surprise, Isabelle had been willing to watch the boys while Nicole went with Kip to get the horses and hitch them up. She suspected it might have something to do with the comment she made at Doreen's on Sunday. As if she suddenly realized what the implications of Nicole's presence would mean to the boys she had grown up with.

Seemed she wasn't as self-centered as she came across.

"I feel like you were railroaded into this," Nicole added, "Are you sure you're comfortable with the idea?"

"I wouldn't be comfortable working with my horses with anyone else," he said, surprising her with his comment.

She tried to read his expression, but he was looking ahead, his eyes shadowed by the brim of his cowboy hat.

"I haven't worked with horses for a while," Kip added. "If things don't go the way I want right off the bat, then we're not doing this at all."

"I understand," Nicole said. "Though I don't have my heart set on going out, I do think it's a good thing for you."

Kip pushed his hat back and glanced at her. "And you care for my welfare because?"

Nicole stopped, looking directly at him. "I care because I saw how much racing those horses meant to you. I care because I have the feeling you're not complete unless you've got a team of horses ahead of you, leather reins threaded through your hands, and the wind in your face."

Kip slowly shook his head, smiling at her. "You seem to spend a lot of time looking out for other people.

Nicole shrugged. "Not really. I just…care."

"Do you ever look out for yourself?"

"Of course I do." Nicole released a short laugh.

"That's why you're doing conference calls on Sunday afternoons and trying to juggle your work at home with your time here."

"It's my reality."

"And you worrying about my mom? Is that your

reality? And the way you're not afraid to tackle Isabelle? And how you're always fussing about the boys?"

Nicole frowned at him. "What are you talking about?"

Kip's expression grew serious. He tapped her on her forehead. "Doesn't this ever get full of other people's things, other people's stuff, other people's problems?"

"I'm not sure…"

Kip released a slow smile. "Of course you're not. And that's part of the problem."

"What problem?" She wasn't sure what he was talking about.

He brushed her cheek with his knuckles, sending a frisson of pleasure up her spine. She gave into an impulse and caught his hand by the wrist.

What are you doing? You're playing with fire.

Nicole dismissed the accusing thoughts. Being with Kip felt right and good. She had never felt this way about any man before, and that had to mean something.

"I get the feeling that you have a hard time thinking about yourself, Nicole Williams. Sometimes I think you should."

His words wound around her heart creating a gentle warmth but she wasn't sure how to reply.

He gave her an enigmatic look, then stepped back.

"Let's go get those horses," Kip said quietly.

Thankfully the horses were already in the corral when they came, so it took no time to bring them into the barn. Nicole held them at the head, while Kip began harnessing. When he had the first buckle done up, the horses sensed what was happening and they stamped and snorted with impatience.

"It's like they missed all of this," Nicole said, steadying the one horse.

Kip grunted as he got out from underneath the horse. "I hope they settle down once we get them going."

He looks worried, Nicole thought.

"I trust you completely," she said quietly.

Kip gave her an enigmatic look then he shook his head lightly. "I sure hope you're right."

The horses danced around, jingling the harnesses, while Kip backed them up to the wagon. A couple of times Nicole was sure he was going to call the whole thing off, but she said nothing, quietly following his instructions, soothing the horses when she could.

"You're pretty good with the horses," Kip said as he clipped and fastened.

"I like horses, and I think they sense that."

"Not many women would feel comfortable handling four horses at the same time," Kip said taking the reins from her. "I've got them now."

Nicole stroked the neck of one of the more

jumpy horses, spoke a few soothing words, then carefully climbed onto the seat of the creaking wooden wagon.

She realized too late that the seat was small and narrow, and she would be sitting right up against Kip.

The horses stamped and tossed their heads, as if eager to get going. Kip climbed onto the wagon, holding the horses back.

"It's been a while since I've taken them out," Kip said as if apologizing for their behavior. His lips were pressed together, and his eyes narrowed. "Last chance," he said adjusting the reins in his hand.

Nicole gave into an impulse, and squeezed his knee. "I'm not worried at all."

Their gazes met and held. Kip lifted the corner of his mouth in a gentle smile. "Thanks for that."

He eased off on the reins, and with a jerk the horses took off, though Kip held them back to a trot.

The wooden wagon had no suspension, and every bump on the ground vibrated up through the wagon seat. That didn't matter. Nicole felt exhilarated watching the four horses move in unison and watching Kip controlling them. He made it look easy, but she could see by the whiteness of his knuckles and the way his elbows locked that he was using a lot of strength to hold them back.

"Why don't you take them onto the tracks?" Nicole suggested. "Maybe they need to get rid of some energy."

Kip shot her a nervous glance. "Are you sure? If they hit the track they'll try to go flat out."

"Like I said, Kip. I trust you to take care of these horses."

Kip drew in a long slow breath then turned the horses toward the beaten oval track on the other side of the horse corral.

As he eased off the reins a bit, one of the leading horses tossed his head and with a jump headed out, the other horses going along.

Nicole grabbed onto the side of the wagon with one hand as the horses gained speed, the beat of their pounding hooves coming closer and closer together. Then they were thundering on the packed ground, manes flying, tails up. Nicole's hair whipped back from her face, and dust roiled around them. Kip narrowed his eyes and leaned forward.

As the horses gained speed, the grin on Kip's face grew wider.

Though she wanted to watch the horses, Nicole could not keep her eyes off him. It was as if he transformed right before her eyes and she saw yet another part of him.

Then, on the second time round the track, she saw Isabelle, Tristan, Justin and Mary standing by the fence watching. Their faces were a blur as they ran past, but she saw the boys waving at them.

They went another time around the track and Kip eased the horses down to a trot, his grin a white flash against his dusty face. "You okay?" he asked Nicole.

"That was fantastic," she said, pushing her hair back from her face.

"Looking good," Mary called out giving him a thumbs-up.

"Can we go for a ride?" Justin yelled.

Kip shook his head. "Nicole and I are taking them out for a bit more. They're still kind of antsy."

Justin pushed his lips out in a pout, Tristan crossed his arms over his chest as if expressing his frustration, but Kip didn't seem moved by the display.

Nicole felt guilty that she was the one to take the first ride out. The grim look on Isabelle's face told Nicole the young girl felt the same. But Mary was grinning. It wasn't hard to see how happy she was to see her son driving the horses again.

"We'll be back in a couple of hours," Kip called out as he eased off on the reins and the horses headed out again, but at a slower pace than before.

Fifteen minutes later, Kip had them eased down to a gentle walk. The creaking of the wagon and the steady plod of the horses hooves filled the silence that sprang up between them.

Nicole was content to simply look around, and enjoy the space and the quiet in his company. That the swaying of the wagon bumped her shoulder up against Kip's from time to time was a nice benefit.

"I'm surprised how much I've missed this," Kip said quietly, finally breaking the silence.

"I can see why. This is beautiful." Nicole's gaze shifted to the mountains edging the field they rode along. "So peaceful. It will be difficult to go back to the city."

Kip sighed lightly and Nicole glanced over at him.

"What's wrong?" she asked.

Kip's only reply was to pull back on the horses, bringing them to a stop. He pushed on what she assumed was the brake of the wagon, then wrapped the reins around the handle of the brake, holding the horses back.

They stamped and snorted, but settled down.

Nicole's heart fluttered in her chest as Kip turned to her. He grazed her cheek with his knuckle, his eyes flitting over her face.

"Do you have to go back?"

Nicole's breath hovered in her chest, as if unsure of where to go.

"You know I do."

"No. I don't." He spoke the words quietly, but Nicole heard an edge of frustration in them.

Her feelings for him were changing every day they spent together. He was easing into a part of her heart that she had kept closed off for a long time, and she sensed he felt the same.

Though it frightened her, it also created tantalizing possibilities, and now he was putting voice to her own questions.

She looked away, her feelings wavering. Staying would make things easier. Staying would be the best solution.

"And what about my father?"

"What about him?"

"He can't be dismissed that easily. He needs to see the boys."

Kip tucked his knuckle under her chin and gently turned her face back to his. "Let's not talk about the boys for now. Let's talk about you and me."

That was even scarier.

"I don't know…"

Kip brushed his knuckle over her skin. "What don't you know? How you feel?"

Nicole pressed her trembling lips together. She knew how she felt about him. She simply didn't dare tell him. Not with so many things hanging between them.

Then Kip leaned closer and brushed a kiss, light as the breeze that toyed with her hair, over her lips. "I think you know how I feel about you."

Nicole caught his hand, hardly daring to think that this man, in spite of who she was, could care for her. Hardly daring to allow herself to take what he was gently offering.

It meant becoming vulnerable and giving Kip the ability to hurt her. To break her heart.

"I'm a stable guy," Kip said, as if reading her thoughts. "I don't say things I don't mean and I do what I say I'm going to do."

Nicole knew that all too well. Taking care of his mother and sister, taking care of the boys. He was stable and sure.

"I don't know how you can," she said quietly, unable to simply take what he was offering. It was a dream. It wasn't possible. "I can't stay. I'm taking the boys—"

Kip silenced her with another kiss. "Don't go," Kip whispered, his lips touching her cheek, her forehead. "Stay here. With me and the boys."

Nicole closed her eyes, his words drawing out her deepest yearnings. Yearnings for a place she belonged. A home. A family.

Oh, how she wanted to give in and say yes.

"You know I care for you," Kip said, pulling

back, his fingers trailing down her cheek. "I think you feel the same way, because I don't think you're the kind of woman who would let someone kiss her casually."

They had only spent a few weeks together and already he knew her that well. "I'm not," she said quietly, clinging to her hands. "You've come to mean more to me than…" she let the sentence trail off, the implications of her words ringing in her mind.

If she acknowledged her true feelings, what would that mean for her? It would tear apart everything she had come here to do.

"I have to bring the boys back to my father."

"Do you really think you can take them away from all of this?" Kip flung his arm out, his movement encompassing the length and breadth of the country surrounding them—the fields, the hills and the mountains beyond that.

His question hit her own doubts with deadly accuracy. She wanted to be able to say without hesitation, yes. Yes, she could.

At one time she'd been able to. But now?

Now she'd seen the boys running free, helping Kip, working with the cows. She could easily see them in the future riding horses once Kip got past his own guilt. She could see them running pell-mell through fields, as free as the horses that Kip raised.

"I don't know," was all she could say.

"Then why do you want to?"

She looked up at him and that was her undoing. Faint lines radiated out from his eyes. Eyes used to squinting against a prairie sun. Eyes that could probe deep into her soul and make her bare secrets she'd told no one.

"I have to. I owe it to my father."

Kip caught her by the shoulders. "Why do you think you owe your father so much? Why do you think his love comes with so many burdens attached to it?"

Nicole wished he weren't holding her. Her own lonely soul yearned for his touch, for his nearness. But she had to explain one more time.

"Sam and Norah took me from a life of uncertainty and gave me security. Gave me a life. They gave me a little sister who I…" Nicole's voice broke on that last word. She fought her tears back. She took a steadying breath. "I owe my father more than I can ever hope to repay."

"And you hope to repay part of that debt by taking the boys away from the only life they'd ever known?"

Nicole wanted to pull away from his touch. It confused her. His hands on her shoulders made her second-guess convictions that weren't as single-minded as they were when she first came.

"Sam gave me a family. He gave me a job. He gave me my life."

"How much is enough to pay that back?"

His words cut her. "How can you ask that?"

"I'm using your language. You're the one talking about owing and repaying."

She didn't know how to answer him.

"Love is a gift, Nicole. It isn't about weighing and measuring and repaying. Love isn't earned. Like the pastor said on Sunday, love is God's great gift to us, and it comes without a price."

"But the boys—"

Kip narrowed his eyes and slowly nodded his head. "It always seems to come back to the boys. I'm wondering if you think bringing them back will earn you your father's love."

Nicole's eyes narrowed. "Is that what you think I'm doing?"

Kip shrugged, pulling away. "Why don't you tell me?"

"It's so much more than that."

"So explain."

"I can't keep the boys away from him, Kip," she snapped, his accusation making her angry. He didn't know. He didn't realize. "I can't. He gave me everything and I took…I sent his only daughter away."

"What? How do you figure that?"

Nicole's anger eased away as her shame, buried

so deep, so long, slowly worked its way through the crack created by her emotions. Like the weeds in the garden she'd been tending with Mary the past few days, the secret was pushing up through and couldn't be hidden.

She bit her lip, looked away, trying to regain the anger. Anger was better. Anger was like an offense. It pushed people away.

But she couldn't find it as easily as she used to.

"Nicole, what are you talking about?" Kip's voice softened and he lifted one hand to cup her cheek.

"I can't...I can't..."

"Please. Tell me."

Nicole took a breath, her own emotions threatening to overwhelm her.

"Tricia...I loved her, you know. She was my sister. My little, adorable, loved and protected sister. She was the daughter that Sam and Norah had waited so long for." She swallowed, struggling to stay on top of her emotions. "She was their only child, but she didn't get it. She didn't understand how good she had it. I tried to tell her. Tried to make her understand. She always fought with our parents. Always rebelled. Then, one day, I found out she'd been hanging out with a bad crowd. Doing drugs. I got mad and yelled at her." The memories came in waves now, relentlessly washing over her. "We had a huge fight. I told her she was treating our parents poorly. She told me that I was jealous of her." Nicole bit her lip and looked down, still ashamed of her actions. "I told her I was. I told her that every day, when I was a little girl, I wished for parents like she had." Nicole clenched her fists, struggling, fighting. "Then I told her she didn't deserve to be a Williams. That she didn't deserve this family and if she couldn't be a loving daughter, if she couldn't appreciate all the good things she'd received from this family, then maybe she should go."

"And then she did leave."

Kip's quiet voice gave substance to the reality that had haunted Nicole from the morning she went to her sister's room.

"She left me a note. Just me." She paused, remembering.

"What did it say?" Kip's gentle voice drew the deeper confession out of her.

"It said that if I thought that our parents were so wonderful, then she was leaving. Leaving me to have them to myself. She told me that she didn't want to be a Williams. That she had never chosen to be a part of this family. That was it. That was the extent of what she wrote." Her voice broke. It was all she could to keep the sorrow inside. "She left because of me. The adopted daughter. The one that was brought into the family. She was the real Williams and she left. I drove her away. I didn't deserve what Sam and Norah had done for me. Sam was right when he told me that. Sam was right when he said that I didn't deserve to be a Williams." A sob crept up her throat and she swallowed it down. "Now Tricia's dead and Norah's dead and I don't know how to fix what I broke. I don't know how except to bring Tricia's boys back. Back to their family…back to Sam…" She stopped as another sob washed upward followed by another. "I owe him so much. He gave me so much, and I'm not even his natural daughter. Bringing the boys back to him will fix everything I did." Suddenly she couldn't hold it back anymore. Sobs racked her body, tears streamed down her cheeks as her shame and pain finally found release.

Next thing she knew she was in Kip's arms and he was holding her tightly against his chest, a haven in the storm of sorrow and pain that she had held back for so long.

"Nicole, oh Nicole, how could you think that?" Kip murmured, his head pressed against hers, his strong arms holding her close.

"I loved them, I did," Nicole sobbed. "I loved them all. But Tricia left and Sam blamed me…I didn't mean to hurt Sam and Norah. I was trying to help. I don't deserve the good things they did for me."

Kip silenced her with another kiss, then he held her close.

"It's not your fault, Nicole. It's not your fault," Kip murmured. "Tricia made her own choices and your father was wrong to drop those choices on your shoulders."

Nicole wanted to believe him. Oh, how she wanted to believe him, but she had clung to that guilt so long, she didn't know if she could let go.

"It's not your fault," Kip repeated, more firmly this time. "You are a good daughter, and you keep saying that you owe Sam Williams. Well, he owes you. You are a faithful daughter. You are a better daughter than Tricia. Any parent would love more than anything to have a daughter as good and faithful as you."

His words eased part of her sorrow. Then he pulled back, framing her face with his hands. "You are an amazing person who has made good choices. You don't need to earn your father's love."

"I didn't really belong—"

"You belong in the Williams family as much as the boys belong in our family." Kip couldn't keep the anger out of his voice. "I don't love those boys more or less because they're not my biological sons. They are a part of me because I chose to take them in. I chose to take them into my heart. They may not have been born to me, but they grew to become a part of me. And I want what's best for them. I want nothing but good things for them."

Nicole heard the conviction in his voice, and her tears slowly subsided and she closed her swollen eyes. Her aching head rested on Kip's shoulder. She didn't want to be strong anymore. She didn't want to be responsible, and she didn't want Kip to let her go.

She stayed there a moment longer, letting his strength hold her up and support her.

He murmured her name again and she looked up at him. His head was a silhouette against the blue prairie sky. Then he lowered his head and his lips touched hers.

She reached up to him, wrapping her arms around him, returning his kiss, letting herself be drawn closer, letting him into her heart.

His lips touched her cheek and then he buried his face in her hair, his one hand caressing her head.

"Don't go, Nicole," he said. "Don't go."

She hardly dared wonder what he was saying. Hardly dared let his words enter her soul.

Instead she stayed in his arms, her own clinging to him, the sun pouring down on them both like a benediction.

She didn't want to go either, but reality seeped into the moment. The boys and the reality of their legal status still stood between them. She knew that she didn't want to take them away from here either. She knew they belonged here.

"We should go back," she said quietly. "I'm sure your mother is wondering what's happening."

"I think she knows." Kip gave her another quick kiss as the wagon jolted. The horses were getting antsy.

Nicole didn't want to go. She wanted this moment to stay forever, this time out of time. She didn't want to go back to the ranch and the boys and the cold, hard reality of the decisions she had to make.

She lowered her arms and drew away.

"Let's go, then."

When they got back to the ranch, Doreen and her kids had arrived, so Kip took the boys and Doreen's kids for a couple of tours around the track while Doreen and Nicole hung over the fence and watched.

"Kip looks good driving the team again," Doreen said quietly, her arms folded over the top rail of the fence.

Nicole wasn't sure what to say in reply, so she just nodded.

"I love watching him with the horses. He hasn't done it for a while and I know he misses it." Doreen's eyes were on Kip, watching his progress around the track, smiling at the sounds of the children's laughter drifting back to them. "Thanks for helping me push him into this."

"I didn't really do much," Nicole protested.

Doreen shot her a wry glance. "You've done more than you might think. I haven't seen Kip this relaxed in a long time." Her voice seemed to hint at something Nicole wasn't sure she wanted to examine. At least not with Kip's sister watching her.

Half an hour later Doreen helped the protesting kids out of the wagon.

"We should go see Grandma," she said as she and Nicole herded the whole works toward the house. "Nicole, you're the horse person. Why don't you help Kip with the horses while I get these kids cleaned up."

And before Nicole could say anything, Doreen was gone, the children trailing behind her.

Thankfully Kip hadn't heard the exchange. She hesitated, but only a moment. The thought of spending more time with Kip was greater than her self-consciousness over what Doreen had hinted at all.

She walked back to where Kip was, helped him lead the horses back to the barn, then helped him unhitch them.

They worked together in silence, but Nicole was aware of every brush of their hands, every time they bumped against each other.

It was like slow torture, she thought. Thankfully, the boys stayed away, letting her and Kip have this moment.

Nicole helped him hang up the harnesses and when everything was done, when there was no job left to do, he turned to her and rested his hands on her arms.

"So, Nicole Williams, where do we go from here?"

She didn't want to think about that. She wasn't sure herself. It made her heart hurt.

Kip's hands lingered on her arms, drifted down to her hands and caught them in hers. The calluses on his hands were rough against hers. The hands of a working man. The hands of a man who cared so much for his family that he was willing to make all the sacrifices that each callus represented.

She chanced a look into his eyes, then brushed her fingers over his cheek, his whiskers rasping against her hand.

"I don't know." She couldn't give him anything more than that. "I simply don't know anymore. The truth is your brother rescued the boys. He saved them when he brought them here."

Kip gave her a sad smile, as if he understood. "They were his boys. What else could he do?"

"But the will. I don't know what to do about the will. If it's proved to be Tricia's…" She wasn't sure where to go anymore. At one time everything was laid out so clearly. Her obligations. Her work. Her plan to bring the boys back to her father where she had, at one time, thought they belonged.

Now it was as if that everything that had given her life meaning was no longer as valid as it had been.

It's not your fault.

Kip's words comforted and frightened her at the same time. Because if Tricia's leaving wasn't her fault, if she was absolved of what Tricia had done, then where did that leave her with her father?

Their entire relationship during the past few years was built on the foundation of Nicole's obligation to her father—first by way of the adoption, then by way of the repercussions of her "talk" with Tricia. The talk that drove Tricia out into the world.

It's not your fault.

"I'm willing to wait," he said quietly. "I'm willing to give you time to sort things out."

His tenderness and consideration cradled her soul.

"You are an amazing man, Kip Cosgrove," she said quietly, squeezing his hand.

Kip's smile created an answering happiness.

Tell him. Tell him that you think the boys should stay.

She held his gaze, wondering what he would

say if she told him that. Wondering what would happen.

Kip's words wound themselves around her weary soul, then his arms held her close. She rested in the shelter they offered, laying her head against his chest, drawing from his quiet strength.

You are a good daughter. You are a good daughter.

She had thought bringing the boys to Toronto could change everything between her and her father, but she also wondered if Kip was right. Was she pinning too much on the boys?

They should stay.

Nicole let the words drift through her mind, testing them.

They belong here.

As Nicole let the words settle, peace entered her soul. And even more important, Kip was offering her something even more.

Did she dare take that too? Wasn't that too many underserved blessings?

And then her phone jangled a tune.

"You were carrying your phone around with you?" Kip laughed.

"I forgot about it," Nicole said with a gentle smile as she pulled the phone out her pocket.

Kip caught her hand. "Just leave it, Nicole. Don't let anything else come in right now."

But as he spoke, her eyes slipped down, as if

they had no power of their own. It was her father calling.

Kip didn't let go of her hand, and as she looked back a him, he didn't let his gaze leave hers as he gently shook his head.

She looked from him to the phone, torn. But years of obligation drew harder on her than her recent moment with Kip.

"I'm sorry. I have to take this." She took a few steps away from him and answered the phone.

"Nicole. Have you spoken to that cowboy's lawyer yet?"

Trust her father to get straight to the point. He must be feeling better, she thought with a measure of relief.

"No, and I don't believe Kip has either."

"You may as well know, we got the first DNA test back today."

"Which one?"

"Mine won't come for a couple of days, but we got Mary Cosgrove's. And we got good news. Mary Cosgrove is not the boys' grandmother."

Nicole pressed her hand to her chest, her emotions in a sudden tailspin. A few weeks ago she would have welcomed this news.

But a few weeks ago, Kip was a hindrance to her goal. A few weeks ago Kip was simply an annoying, attractive complication getting in the way of her plan to take the boys back to where she thought they belonged.

How much had changed in the past week. The past few days.

Nicole didn't want to let her mind dwell on that. Her father's phone call and the hard reality of the boys' parentage were what she had to face now.

She tried not to look at Kip, refocussing her emotions. She knew her father well enough to understand what his next step would be.

"So that means..."

"Scott Cosgrove is not the boys' father. The boys belong to me. I want you to bring them back here as soon as possible. I've got the lawyer coming tomorrow afternoon. He's filing the papers and after that I want the boys back here."

"How can you—"

"I'll use the police if I have to," Sam growled.

Nicole rubbed her forehead with her fingers. He would, she thought. Once Sam Williams had an idea in his head, there was no stopping him no matter how he felt.

Nicole glanced back at Kip, who was watching her. Again her obligations to her father pulled on her.

She looked away from him. She had to make a choice. Had to make a decision.

But how could she go through with it?

Chapter Fifteen

Kip watched the interplay of emotions on Nicole's face while she spoke to her father on the phone.

Panic shot through him when her eyes widened and she glanced at Kip. The expression on her face wasn't encouraging.

Then she walked away from him, talking in low, urgent tones.

He wanted to grab the phone out of her hands and tell her to put her father aside. To put the boys aside. To focus on what she needed and wanted.

Kip stood, his hands on his hips, watching as she wilted in front of his eyes. Her shoulders dropped, her head lowered and she seemed to turn in on herself.

Did she even realize what effect her father had on her?

A few minutes later she was finished with her call. She stood with her back to him, her head lowered, and Kip felt as if everything he'd told her had been erased with that one phone call.

She turned back to him and he read the anguish on her face.

"I have to go back," she said quietly.

Kip started. This was not what he expected to hear. "Go back? To Toronto? Is something wrong with your father?"

She shook her head. "He's feeling much better." She bit her lip and Kip's heart dropped into his gut.

"So why do you have to go back now? Just as things are changing for us?"

"I know, but…" She lifted her hands toward him, then clenched them into fists. "The situation is different."

"How? What did your father say to you that could possibly have made such a difference?"

Nicole pressed her fists against her forehead. Kip wanted to drag her hands away and tell her how much he hated seeing her like this.

Nicole lowered her hands, but still didn't look at him. "My father got the first of the DNA tests back."

Kip's breath left him in a rush. His heart vibrated erratically, like it always did before a big race when he thought about the uncertainty of what lay ahead and where events would take him.

At least, when he was racing, he had the reins in his hand. He was in charge.

"There were no DNA matches between the boys and your mother. From what the lab could figure out, Scott wasn't the boys' biological father."

Kip could only stare at her. It was as if her mouth was moving but he couldn't figure out exactly what she was saying. Something about Scott not being the boys' father? "How…how can that be? That's impossible."

Ron was supposed to have heard about the tests the same time as Mr. William's lawyer. Why hadn't Ron called him?

"Why would Scott…he mustn't have known…" Kip's voice drifted off as the implications of this slowly sank in.

"It was what I had told you from the beginning," she said.

Kip could only stare at her. Was that all she had to say? "Are you kidding me?"

Nicole frowned as if she didn't understand. "Kip, why is this such a surprise? I told you that Tricia said—"

"And Scott told me they were his kids." Kip shoved his hand through his hair and spun away from her. He couldn't pull his thoughts together into a coherent sentence.

When Nicole had first come with her far-fetched story of the boys not belonging to Scott, he'd never, for one moment, believed her.

His thoughts sped back and forth as he tried to think. To plan.

"She left them," he growled, his pain and frustration seeping into his voice. "She abandoned those boys and Scott saved them." He turned back to her. "That has to mean something."

Nicole didn't reply.

"He did what he was supposed to, even if the boys weren't his. Nicole, tell me what you're thinking." He wanted to pull her close. He wanted to go back to where they were before her father intruded into her life again. "Tell me what's on your mind."

She reached out and touched his face, her cool fingers trailing a light caress down his cheek. "I have to go," she said quietly.

"Don't do this, Nicole," Kip said. "Don't throw what we have away."

She took a step back.

Away from him.

"Don't go, Nicole. Don't make me your enemy."

She gave him a sad smile. "You'll never be my enemy."

"If you try to take my boys away, you will be. I'll fight you tooth and nail for them."

As soon as the words left his mouth, he regretted saying them. It wasn't about the boys. It was about her. He didn't want her to go. He didn't want to lose her.

But he wasn't sure he could say that yet.

She paused, the hurt in her eyes obvious. Then she turned and walked away.

This wasn't where they were supposed to end up, but he didn't know how to get back to where he wanted to be.

Go after her. Don't let her leave you like this. Tell her how you really feel.

He took a step toward her, then stopped himself. No. She had made her choice. In spite of everything he had told her, everything he had offered her, she'd chosen her father over him.

He had to stay back here and fight for his boys and let her go back to where she thought she belonged.

"I'm sorry, I don't have the best news, Kip," Ron said.

Kip clutched the telephone, glancing over at his mother, who stood by the sink, peeling potatoes.

Since Nicole had left two days ago, his mother had been working harder and harder on her exercises. It was as if she wanted to get strong enough to stand up for her grandsons.

But they're not her grandsons.

Kip pushed the traitorous thought away. The boys were as much a part of his family as they were part of the Williams family. More, in fact.

"They've filed for legal custody of the boys." Ron's voice was a disembodied sound as Kip realized what had happened. No wonder she took off so quick.

After Nicole had left, some part of him had nurtured the faintest hope that she would come back and tell him she had changed her mind.

But he heard nothing. No phone call, no email. Just a long, frustrating silence that grew more oppressing each day. A silence that choked off the brief moment of enthusiasm he'd experienced when he hitched up the horses.

A silence that slowly eroded at the hope she would come back and tell him she would help him fight for the boys.

Instead she had chosen her father over them.

What did you expect? A few kisses and a few declarations of affection and she was going to throw over nearly a lifetime of obligation to a man who required more than she could give?

"So what do we do now?" Kip asked, fear and frustration and confusion warring in his gut.

"We can fight back," Ron said. "Claim that Scott acted in the best interests of the boys when he took them. I'm still working on the validity of her will, but I'm warning you, it's uphill now that it's been proven the boys aren't Scott's."

Kip sighed and tunneled his hand through his hair.

"So what do you want me to do?" Ron pressed.

"I can't think right now. I'll have to get back to you." Kip disconnected the phone and released a heavy sigh.

"I take it that's not good news," Mary said, her voice small.

Kip glanced her way, wondering how much to tell her. "Nicole's father has filed for custody of the boys." Kip said, preferring to break things to his mother one piece of bad news at a time.

His mother flipped her tea towel over her shoulder and came to sit beside him. "What are we going to do?"

"I don't think there's anything we can do," Kip said. "I'm sure that's why Nicole hightailed it back to Toronto so fast. She didn't want to be around when everything imploded."

Mary laid her hand on his arm. "I know that you cared for her," his mother said quietly.

Kip sighed. "Yeah. I did."

"Did?" his mother pressed.

"Do." He tapped his fingers on his arm. "I don't know what to do. Don't know what to think."

"Why?"

Kip held his mother's gaze, then looked past her to the kitchen with its worn cupboards, stained linoleum and scarred countertop. He had only seen pictures of the outside of Nicole's home, but he was sure the countertops were granite, the floor solid hardwood and the cupboards crafted from some exotic wood that he'd never heard of.

"Even before Nicole came, I often wondered how I would take care of everyone." He hated to admit this to his mother, but he had to be honest with her. "I wondered especially about the boys. Would I be able to give them the life I thought they should have." He looked up at her. "I don't think I can give them the life that I know the Williams family can."

His mother gave him a tired smile. "I know how you feel. I've thought the same."

Her admission gave Kip some measure of relief. At least he didn't feel like he was giving up on the boys.

"You've taken on a lot since your father died. You've always taken everything on yourself." Mary put her hand on his shoulder. "Now you've got the boys."

"Not for long, it seems."

He caught a glimmer of tears in his mother's eyes. "I don't want to see them go either, but you can only do so much." She caught his hands in her own, turning them over. "We've all depended on you a lot. Depended on you to take care of us. To do what needed to be done. Then Nicole came and it was as if a burden shifted off your shoulders. She seemed to take some of what you were carrying on herself. The boys, me. Even Isabelle." She released a short laugh and squeezed his hands. "What is more important, I saw you smile. I saw you happy. I saw you falling in love again. That hasn't happened in a long time."

"I was in love with Nancy."

Mary shrugged. "I never saw you smile at Nancy the way I see you smile at Nicole, and I never saw you as upset about Nancy leaving the way you have been since Nicole left."

Kip eased out another sigh.

"I don't know what to do, Mom."

His mother squeezed his hands. "You can't 'do' anything anymore. Now, I think you have to let go and let God."

The familiar adage had always seemed lame and empty, but now, in the face of a situation that Kip could not control, he knew he had to do exactly what his mother suggested.

"Can we pray together?" his mother asked.

He nodded and together they bowed their heads.

"Please Lord, You know what is in our hearts. You know that we are concerned over what will happen to our boys, but at the same time, You know better what they need. Help us to trust that You will take care of them. Help us to realize that they were Yours before they were ever ours. Amen."

Before he raised his head, Kip added his own prayer for Nicole. For his own feelings for her. Because right now he was having a harder time putting her into God's hands than he was the boys.

Chapter Sixteen

⁓❧

The room was everything a little boy could want and, Nicole guessed, no expense was spared. Nicole adjusted the pillows of the bed, shaped like a car, then eased out a sigh. The past couple of days she'd felt as if she were hurtling down a road she had no control over.

I can do all things through him who strengthens me.

The verse of the Bible resonated through Nicole's mind. Since arriving here, she had found an old Bible of her mother's. She had brought it into her room and read it whenever she had the chance. Yesterday she had read this quote.

Nicole clung to the words. She knew she would need the encouragement she had gotten from reading that in the next couple of days.

She gently closed the door of the large room and walked down the carpeted hall and down the stairs, her hand trailing over the wooden banister. Tricia used to slide down it, but Nicole never dared be that rebellious.

She glanced around the large foyer with its sparkling chandelier and windows that stretched up two and a half floors. Her mind slipped back to the jumbled porch of the Cosgrove household, the worn flooring in the kitchen and the faded paint on the outside of the house. In spite of the general air of neglect, that house felt more like a home than this house ever did.

Her heart faltered. Though she had been gone from the ranch only two days, it seemed like two weeks. She hadn't dared call Kip, but he had not called her either.

She missed him so much it hurt her heart. She wondered what he was thinking right now. She wondered if he thought of her. If he missed her as much as she missed him.

She wanted to talk to him, and chances were good she would one way or the other. The boys still had to be dealt with. But before she talked to Kip, she had to try one more thing.

Please Lord, help me through this, she prayed, one hand clutching the wooden banister. Then she took a breath, and strode down the long hallway to the sun room where her father waited for her.

"What do you think of the changes I've made

for the boys?" Sam asked, looking up as she came into the room.

Her father sat in a wicker chair, his cheeks shining and his eyes bright. He looked better than he had in months.

And no wonder. He had a project and a purpose. Making plans and getting the house ready for Tricia's boys, as he'd been calling them since Nicole came back. He'd already managed to find a school they could attend come fall and had looked into various sports programs they would be able to participate in.

He was like a one-man freight train, pulling everyone along.

"I love the playroom, and I'm sure they would too," Nicole said quietly, settling into the padded wicker love seat across from her father.

"Would?" Of course Sam would have caught that tiny slip of the tongue. "What do you mean by that?"

Nicole wound a loose thread around the button on her cardigan, inarticulate words and thoughts piling up in her mind as she tried to sort out how to voice them.

She was about to speak when her father gestured to the pile of envelopes sitting on the table between them. "Heather brought this for you to look at."

Nicole frowned. "I had asked Heather to take care of the mail at the office."

"Heather did mention something like that when I asked her to bring it." Her father frowned. "You know all the ins and outs of the foundation's correspondence better than she ever will."

"I won't always be around," Nicole said, trying to lead into one of the things she wanted to talk to her father about.

"Nonsense. You're my right-hand man."

I would prefer to be your daughter, Nicole thought.

Instead she picked up the mail and started sorting through it.

She glanced at the return address of a large envelope, wondering what this was about. The corner was emblazoned with the name of a clinic that was unfamiliar to her.

She held up the envelope. "What's this?" she asked. "Test results?"

Her father looked up from the papers he was going over, then nodded. "I think that's the DNA test I had to do. The same test that messed up the expectations of that Cosgrove family."

Nicole's heart beat heavy in her chest at the contempt in her father's voice.

"That test didn't mess up that family that much," Nicole murmured, struggling against years of training that taught her to never, ever talk back to her father either as father or boss.

"What do you mean?" her father growled, then began coughing.

Nicole jumped to her feet and handed him a glass of water. He took the glass, took a drink, then stared up at Nicole. "They thought they had a biological claim on the boys, but they didn't. We won." He coughed again and took another drink.

Nicole put the glass back, then returned to her seat. She picked up the letter and stared at it. "Won what?" she asked.

"What is going on with you? Ever since you came back from Alberta you've been distracted. Like your mind is somewhere else."

It was, Nicole thought, slitting opening the envelope with her father's silver letter opener. Her mind was with Kip and Tristan and Justin and Kip and Mary...and Kip.

"I think you need to do something other than foundation work this afternoon," her father said. "Why don't you go out to one of those toy places and buy some kind of jungle gym for the yard," her father said. "Get something for the boys to play on."

Nicole glanced through the windows of the sun room to the yard beyond. Though it was large by Toronto standards, it suddenly looked small and restrictive compared to what she knew Tristan and Justin were used to.

"Would they love it?" she asked.

"What do you mean?"

Nicole pulled the letter slowly out of the envelope, still staring at the yard. "The only place those boys have known is the ranch. I wonder what it will be like for them to be uprooted from that."

Her father waved his hand, as if erasing her concerns. "You said yourself the Cosgroves were broke."

"I never said that. I said it didn't look like they had an abundance of ready cash." Which, when they thought the Cosgrove family might be willing to fight them in court, had been a concern.

"You know we can give the boys a better life."

"In one way, yes we can, but I don't think it's a good idea to uproot them."

Her father almost snorted. "You were moved around a lot and you turned out fine. Because we gave you a better place than any of the places you lived before. We gave you the best home you ever had."

Something that had been pointed out to her daily.

Something that never happened at the Cosgrove home. Tristan and Justin would grow up never knowing what Kip had sacrificed to be a father to them and to give them a home.

She thought of his chuck-wagon racing and her mind ticked back to her ride with him. How his eyes, no, his entire face lit up with excitement and the pure pleasure of working with the horses. He gave all that up for the boys, but she never got any sense of regret from Kip.

She riffled the papers in her hand, forcing herself to meet her father's piercing gaze. "I'm not sure we can do the same for Tristan and Justin," she said, quietly.

"What do you mean?"

Nicole kept her eyes on his, putting voice to the uncertainties that had grown in intensity in the past week. Uncertainty that had grown into a reality. "I'm not sure we can give them a better home than they have in Alberta. I think they have everything they will ever want or need there. They belong in Alberta. With the Cosgroves."

"What are you talking about?" Her father looked baffled, as if he wasn't sure he had heard her properly.

"They've lived with that family for four years. They are the only family they know." Nicole's voice faltered as she tried to articulate what she had to say.

"What does that matter? Those boys don't even belong to them. Never will, no matter what they may think. They belong here. They belong to me. They're my only daughter's sons."

Only daughter. Why, after all this time, could those words still hurt so much?

Because she'd seen something else. She'd seen

another kind of love. A kind of love that didn't depend on biology. The kind of love that was pure gift.

Just like God's love.

"I don't think Tristan and Justin belong to anybody," Nicole said carefully. "We have been treating them like they are possessions. They are people. Little boys, who only know what it's like to live on a ranch, with wide-open spaces, an uncle who loves them and a huge family who cares for them deeply. I think it's selfish to take them away from all of that."

"Are you saying I'm selfish for wanting to have my daughter's children living with me? Especially after this is what she wanted?" Her father's voice rose with each question, as if he could hardly believe that she would question him.

Please Lord, help me find the right words, she prayed. Sam is still my father.

"I think we have to step back from the situation, and forget about what Tricia wanted, what we want, I think we need to look at the boys' situation for their sake, not ours."

"Are you daring to question me?" Her father struggled to his feet, staring at her as if she didn't understand who he was talking to. "What kind of daughter does that?"

For a moment remorse clung to her.

You're a good daughter. You're a good daughter.

Kip's words resonated through her mind, washing away the guilt her father could so easily resurrect in her.

Love does not delight in evil, but rejoices with the truth.

She clung to those words as she turned to her father.

"The kind of daughter who thinks she should tell the truth. I can't support you in your fight to bring the boys back here. I can't help you with that and I won't."

Her father stared at her, as if he didn't recognize her. "Are you saying you would fight me?"

"I'm saying I would fight for what is best for Tristan and Justin," she amended. "If that puts me against you, then that's they way it has to be."

"You would choose that family over me?"

"It's not about choosing, Father. It's about doing what's best for the boys."

Sam's eyes narrowed and his expression grew thunderous. "After everything I've done for you, after all I've given you, this is how you repay me?"

"Repay you?" Nicole spoke quietly. "I didn't think love came with a cost."

Her father looked taken aback, but changed

tactics. "You've done much damage to this family—"

"Tricia made her own choices, Father," Nicole said quietly, drawing on the words Kip had told her. Words she had held close in the past few days.

"You pushed her."

"You pushed her too," Nicole snapped back. Her outburst surprised her as much as it surprised her father judging from the shocked look on his face. "I think she was leaving regardless. My fight with her was simply bad timing," she continued, suddenly tired of her father's endless condemnation.

In the shocked silence that followed Nicole's outburst she looked down at the letter she still held in her hands. She skimmed over the words, giving herself something to do other than face her father's anger. She came to the end of the letter.

What in the world?

She read it one more time, to make sure she had read correctly.

"What's wrong?" her father asked, obviously distracted by her puzzlement. "What's in the letter?"

She cleared her throat and looked at her father. "It says that the DNA from you doesn't match the boys', either."

Sam snatched the papers from her hand, his eyes racing over the letter. Then again. "I don't understand." He looked up, his once ruddy face, ashen. "The boys didn't belong to that man Tricia was living with and we know they are Tricia's. The detective's reports showed that."

Nicole frowned. "Detective's reports?"

"I hired a private detective to find a few more things out about Tricia and Scott."

This was news to her. Not that it mattered anymore. Now they were faced with an entirely different puzzle.

Sam looked down at the papers, shaking his head. "I don't understand. I simply don't..." His voice faded as he read the papers again, his hands clenching.

Then his face grew hard, his eyes glinted and his nostrils flared as his head moved back and forth as if in denial of facts he couldn't absorb.

He flung the papers to the ground, glaring at them.

"Norah, how could you?" he called out.

"What are you talking about?" Nicole asked, catching him by the arm. "What's going on?"

He spun to face her, his eyes glittering with anger, his breath coming in short spurts. "I should have confronted her. But no. I thought Norah and that Bart fellow were just friends."

Nicole's confusion grew with every word. "I don't know what you mean. I don't know who Bart is."

Her father looked everywhere but at her as he seemed to gather his thoughts. He took a few breaths, then, as if the life was sucked out of him, his shoulders sagged down, his head lowered.

"Just before we adopted you, we found out I wasn't able to father a child. But Norah wanted a child so badly. I didn't. Then she started spending time with Bart and his wife. Finally, I gave in and she adopted you. Then, a few years later, when Norah had Tricia, it was like a miracle. That happens sometimes." His hands trembled as he dragged them over his face. "She told me Bart was just a friend and I believed her. Turns out, if this report is true, it seems he was a whole lot more."

"You can't know that for sure," Nicole said, stroking his shoulder, her pity for him coming to the fore.

"I always suspected." Sam pushed at the papers with the toe of his slipper. "This proves it." He stumbled back to his chair and dropped his head in his hands. "How could she have done this to me?" Her father sighed, then looked up at Nicole. "If my DNA doesn't match the boys, then this means that Tricia isn't my daughter either."

The "either" was like a small, indifferent slap.

"That means those boys don't belong to me."

Nicole was set back on her heels, trying to absorb everything she'd heard in the past few minutes. Tricia not her father's biological daughter. Her mother cheating on her father?

She couldn't put it all together.

Sam sighed, pushing his hands through his hair. "Tricia wasn't my daughter. She wasn't my daughter and I raised her. Paid for everything she had. What a waste."

On one level Nicole felt sorry for him and tried to realize that he was speaking from his pain, but on another level his words underlined the insecurity she'd felt ever since coming to this family.

He had paid for everything she had done. Was she a waste too?

Sam took another breath, then straightened and looked directly at Nicole. "So you said you would fight me over those boys?"

Puzzled as to where he was going with this, Nicole could only nod.

"You would really choose them over me?"

"It's not a matter of choice, but if that's how you want to put it, then I would put their needs over yours because I think Kip Cosgrove is the best person to be taking care of those boys." She still wasn't sure what was going on, but she stuck to what she knew to be right and true.

Sam emitted a bitter laugh. "That cowboy? What could he possibly give them?"

Anger surged through Nicole at the contempt in his voice and she stepped away from her father.

"That cowboy has made more sacrifices for Tristan and Justin than you ever have for me or Tricia. That cowboy is a kind and considerate man who I respect more than I've ever respected any man, including you. That cowboy is the best example of a father's love that I could ever imagine. I'm jealous of those boys because that cowboy is the best thing that has ever happened to them. Right now I wish I was with Kip, that cowboy as you call him, instead of here with you."

Her father stared at her, then he got up and walked over to the papers that still lay on the floor. He bent over and picked them up. Then he glanced over her shoulder.

"Looks like you might get your wish after all," was all he said.

What did he mean?

Nicole felt a prickling at the back of her neck, then slowly turned around. Her eyes widened.

How did he...? When...?

Kip stood in the doorway of the sun room, his cowboy hat pulled low on his head, his hands on his jeans-clad hips. She blinked, wondering if she was imagining things.

As she tried to pull her mind around his presence, her father grabbed the papers and walked over to Kip.

"You want those boys?" he asked. Then, without waiting for an answer, Sam Williams shoved the papers into Kip's hands. "You can have them. They don't belong to me."

Kip glanced from Sam to Nicole as he took the papers, his expression unreadable. Then he looked back at Sam. "Those boys don't belong to me either."

"What do you mean by that? I thought you wanted them."

"I do, but they aren't a possession, just like Nicole isn't your possession. The boys are a gift, like Nicole is a gift."

Sam glanced back over his shoulder, frowning as if trying to see her that way.

Then, without a backward glance, he walked slowly over to his office and closed the door behind him.

Nicole clasped her suddenly trembling hands together, still trying to absorb his presence in her home.

Kip took off his hat, and glanced around the sun room. "So this is a nice place you have here," he said.

"What are you doing here?" Nicole asked.

He took a few steps closer and dropped his hat on the chair beside her. Then his warm rough hands were covering hers. "I could be all manly and say I've come to claim what's mine. That might be partly true, but mostly I came because I wanted to see you."

Nicole closed her eyes, as if by doing so she could better absorb what he was saying. Then his lips brushed her forehead and her eyes flew open.

"Did you mean what you said to your father before I came in?" he asked, his voice quiet, but intense.

Nicole clung to his hands, her gaze clinging to his. "Every word."

He squeezed her hands. "I spent half the flight here practicing what I would say. I even wrote it down so I wouldn't forget." He took in a long, slow breath and blew it out, as if gathering his strength. "I want you to know that whatever you decide about Tristan and Justin has nothing to do with how I feel about you. I want what's best for the boys, and if you and your mother think that having them here is best for them, I'm willing to go with that."

Nicole could only stare at him, his speech in direct contrast to what she had just heard from her own father.

"You would give up the boys?" she asked.

"Like I told your father, I think I've had to realize they aren't mine, or yours or his to give up. But I do have to let go of what I want and put their needs first."

Nicole could only stare. This amazing, wonderful, caring man was willing to do something her father couldn't even conceive of doing. "Why?"

"Because I love them."

Back to love again.

"Because they are God's children first," Kip continued, "When I think that, I realize that what they need is more important than what I want."

"That's amazing," was all she could say.

"Not really." He blew out his breath, his hands kneading hers. Then he cleared his throat and continued. "I also want you to know that I care for you more than I ever cared for anyone. I don't know how it happened, and I don't know why, but for some reason I seem to have fallen in love with you."

Nicole's throat thickened with emotion as she stared at Kip. This wonderful, loving and caring man had fallen in love with her? She couldn't absorb it, couldn't take it in. It was too much.

Kip inclined his head toward her and gave a nervous laugh. "Usually a declaration like that requires some kind of response."

Happiness and gratitude and love washed over her in a cleansing flood. She fought back tears as she slipped her arms around his neck, pulled him toward her, and pressed a firm kiss to his lips. Then she drew back, her fingers tangling in his hair, then tracing the contours of his face as if making sure he was really here and really telling her all these wonderful things. "I've fallen in love with you too." Her words came out a lot shakier than his as she blinked away unexpected tears. "I can't believe that this is happening."

"Me neither." Kip kissed her again pulling her close to him. "I didn't know how this would turn out," he murmured stroking her hair as he tucked her head against his shoulder. "I only knew I couldn't stay on the ranch one moment longer without letting you know how I felt about you. I need you in my life. I need you at my side."

Nicole's heart could hold no more happiness. "I need you too," she murmured. "The past two days have been so hard. I needed to talk to my father, to try to convince him that the boy should stay where they are."

Kip kissed her again. "I don't want to talk about the boys right now. They've been too much a part of all of this. In spite of what I said before, my main reason for coming here was for you, and only you."

Nicole's first thought was that she didn't deserve such happiness. Maybe she didn't, but that didn't matter. It was being given to her, freely and without strings attached.

She kissed Kip again. "I love you so much," she whispered, stroking his face. "Though you didn't come here to talk about the boys, you may as well know that I believe my father is repealing his claim to them."

"Why would he be willing to give them up without a fight?"

"He just found out that his DNA doesn't match the boys' either."

Kip frowned. "I'm not sure I follow."

Nicole smiled at him. "Given the way my father operates, I think once he found out that the boys weren't biologically his, they didn't mean as much to him." She paused, biting her lip. "That's important to him."

Kip stroked her arms, his eyes narrowing. "I said this before, and I'll say it again, that man was blessed beyond blessing to have you as his daughter. He doesn't deserve you."

Kip's heartfelt words pierced her soul, and made a home there.

"Of course I don't deserve you either," he continued. "But I'm hoping I can persuade you to come back to the ranch." Kip's smile was tentative, as if he didn't dare believe she would take him up on the offer. "And once you're back in Alberta, I'm hoping I can persuade you to marry me."

Nicole threw her arms around Kip's neck her heart bursting with love. "I won't take much convincing. In fact, I've already got my suitcases packed."

Kip stared at her openmouthed. "For what?"

"Before you came, I was going to tell my father that I'm moving out. I didn't get the chance once the letter came. And then you came and now…"

"You should tell him now and I'm coming with you." Kip kissed her again. "I have a few things I have to discuss with him too."

Nicole opened the door of her father's office. Sam stood at the window, looking out over the yard, his shoulders slumped, his hands clasped behind his back.

Was he imagining Justin and Tristan playing there? Was he regretting the loss of the dreams and plans he had made?

Then he turned and simply stared at them as if waiting for them to talk.

"I've come to say goodbye," Nicole said quietly. "I meant to tell you earlier, but I'm moving out."

Sam glared at Kip, as if he was to blame. "And what about him?"

Kip stepped forward, his hat in his hand. A sign of respect, Nicole thought. He really was a good man.

"I want to let you know that I've asked Nicole to marry me. She's coming back to Alberta with me now. We will notify you of the wedding date." His words came out clipped, precise. As if he was making some kind of business deal.

"Aren't you supposed to ask my permission? I am after all her father."

"That's good to know," Kip said quietly.

"What's that supposed to mean?" Sam asked with a frown. But he didn't give Kip a chance to answer. He turned to Nicole. "I don't deserve to be treated like this."

Kip laid his arm over her shoulder and squeezed, encouraging her. Nicole gave him a quick smile, then walked over to her father's side.

"Someone told me once that I was a good daughter," she said quietly. "I believe them now. I've always tried to earn your love, but I'm not doing that anymore. Love is a gift. Kip taught me that," she said glancing over her shoulder at the man she loved. "I'll always love you, and I'll always be thankful for the family you've given me. However, it's time for me to start my own family." She gave her father a kiss. "I've left instructions to the housekeeper about what is supposed to happen with the things I couldn't take along. If there's any problem, let me know and I'll call you once I'm back in Alberta." Her father didn't reply. Nicole then turned and walked back to Kip, taking his hand in hers.

A few minutes later they walked out of the large double doors to a small car waiting outside.

"You couldn't get a truck?" Nicole asked as Kip opened the trunk and dropped her suitcases inside.

"This was all they had left at the airport," Kip said. "Once we're back in Alberta, I'll have my truck back again. And it can't come too soon." He shuddered. "Driving in Toronto is like pulling out my fingernails. Slowly."

Nicole could imagine. "Do you want me to drive back to the airport?"

"That's a direct affront to my masculinity," Kip said as he slammed the trunk shut. He jingled his keys as he looked up at the house. "Are you sure you won't miss all this?"

Nicole glanced behind her at the place that had been her home for the most of her life, trying to see it through Kip's eyes.

It was imposing compared to the farmhouse, but it was simply bricks piled upon bricks. Just a house.

"I might, just a bit," she said quietly, then turned back to Kip and smiled. "I think what I'll miss the most is having my own housekeeper."

"We could always put up a notice advertising for one at the local post office," Kip said with a grin, as he helped her into the car.

"Are you kidding?" Nicole said, wrinkling her nose. "You never know who'll show up on your doorstep."

"No, you don't," Kip said dropping a kiss on her forehead. "But you never know what might come of it."

Nicole cast another glance over her shoulder at the place that had been her home. Then she got into the car and turned to Kip.

"And now, let's go home."

Epilogue

"C'mon. Let's go. C'mon," Kip yelled, slapping his reins on the backs of the horses, squinting into the dust raised by dozens of hooves pounding into the ground and sixteen wagon wheels churning up the dirt.

Yokes clanked, wheels rumbled and above all that he could hear the roar of the crowd as his horses stretched out, doing the best and gaining foot by foot.

Just a bit more. Just a few feet more and they'd be ahead of the leader, Willard Kelly.

Kip braced himself against the rocking of the wagon, leaning ahead as far as he dared urging his horses on. The spectators lining the rails were a blur. Kip knew Nicole and the boys were watching, but he kept his focus on the horses and on the finish line.

A bit more. Just a bit more.

Then they were across the chalked line and the race was over.

Kip drew back on the reins, pulling his horses back. They tossed their heads, unwilling to stop. They had done well, he thought. They had done their best and he was thrilled they had come this far.

The Rangeland Derby. Even to qualify had been thrill enough for him.

"And the winner of the heat, back in competition after a long break...Kip Cosgrove."

The words of the announcer blared above the noise of the crowd and Kip dropped back onto the seat of the chuck wagon, his heart pounding.

He won his heat. He actually won his heat.

The reins slipped through his hand because of his moment of inattention and he gathered them up, slowly bringing his horses to a quick walk.

He'd won his heat. And, even better, he won in front of Nicole and the kids.

"Good race, Kip," Willard called out as he turned his team around. "Good to see you back on the circuit."

Kip nodded his acknowledgement, his entire focus on getting his horses turned around. The next group of wagons were coming around for their heat and he needed to get out of the way.

When he got his horses turned, his sponsor's

rep, Aidan Thomson, jumped into his wagon to join him in the victory walk past the stands.

"Good race, Cosgrove," he said, slapping Kip on the shoulder, then waving to the people as they drove past the grandstand. "Your father-in-law will be happy to know he's getting a return on his sponsorship."

Kip just grinned, rubbed the dust out of his eyes with his arm and glanced over the people gathered at the rail.

Then he saw them. Nicole waving, Justin sitting on the rail whistling, Tristan yelling with his hands cupped around his mouth.

Mary and Isabelle stood to one side madly waving as well. On Nicole's other side stood Nicole's father, arms resting on the rails, eyes narrowed as if still trying to figure this whole chuck-wagon-racing thing out.

Sam gave Kip a curt nod of his head, and from Sam Williams that was high praise indeed.

Sam had kept his distance for a while until Kip's mother had taken things in hand and called him. She'd told him in no uncertain terms he could either die a lonely, miserable old man or he could accept the family he had and see it as a blessing.

It had taken a few letters, a few pictures and a few phone calls from Nicole for Sam to come around. But eventually he had. During his first visit to the ranch, the twins had been enthusiastic and charming and he had thawed under their spell. Seeing Kip working with the horses had sealed the deal and Kip had gotten a new sponsor.

Then Kip caught Nicole's gaze.

She pressed her fingers to her mouth and blew him a kiss, grinning and waving. I love you, she mouthed.

I love you, too, he returned.

"Nice little family you got there," Aidan said.

"The best," Kip said, bunching his reins into one hand and waving back, his grin almost hurting his face. "The best family this cowboy could ask for."

* * * * *

Dear Reader,

The burden of obligation can lie heavily on someone's shoulders. Especially when carrying that burden makes a person feel they are less. Nicole struggled with the fact that she was adopted, and therefore she felt an obligation to earn the love of her parents. And to some degree, her father reinforced that idea. Kip, in spite of his own shortcomings, was an example to her of love that gives without expectation of a return. The kind of love that God gives us every day. I know there are times that I don't feel I deserve God's love. That I have to earn it and work for it. But the reality is that God's perfect love cannot be earned. It can only be received. I pray that you may feel God's awesome, powerful love in your life as well.

Carolyne Aarsen

QUESTIONS FOR DISCUSSION

1. What did you think was Nicole's main reason for wanting to bring the boys back?

2. What was your opinion of Kip's reaction to what she wanted to do?

3. Have you ever been in a situation like Nicole where you felt you had to earn love?

4. Was Kip right in wanting to keep the boys with him even though he might not be their biological uncle. Why or why not?

5. Have you ever had an experience with adoption?

6. What should have been Nicole and Kip's main priority?

7. Many times in our own lives we can feel that God doesn't care. Have you ever had a situation like that?

8. What was your reaction to the sacrifices Kip made for his family? Why do you think he made them?

9. What was your reaction to how Sam felt about the boys once he found out that Tricia wasn't his biological daughter? Could you sympathize?

10. Nicole ended up having to make a choice. How did you feel about her choice? Do you think she was justified in standing up to her father? What would you have done in her situation?

LARGER PRINT BOOKS!

GET 2 FREE LARGER PRINT NOVELS PLUS 2 FREE MYSTERY GIFTS

Love Inspired®

Larger print novels are now available...

YES! Please send me 2 FREE LARGER PRINT Love Inspired® novels and my 2 FREE mystery gifts (gifts are valued at $10). After receiving them, if I don't wish to receive any more books, I can return the shipping statement marked "cancel." If I don't cancel, I will receive 3 brand-new novels every month and be billed just $4.74 per book, a savings of $1.51 off the cover price, plus 25¢ shipping and handling per book and applicable taxes, if any*. I understand that accepting the 2 free books and gifts places me under no obligation to buy anything. I can always return a shipment and cancel at any time. Even if I never buy another book from Steeple Hill, the two free books and gifts are mine to keep forever.

101 IAN EYP2

Name	(PLEASE PRINT)	
Address		Apt. #
City	State	Zip

Signature (if under 18, a parent or guardian must sign)

Mail to Steeple Hill Reader Service:
P.O. Box 1867, Buffalo, NY 14240-1867

Are you a current Love Inspired subscriber and want to receive the larger print edition?

Call 1-800-873-8635 today!

* Terms and prices subject to change without notice. Prices do not include applicable taxes. Sales tax applicable in N.Y. This offer is limited to one order per household. All orders subject to approval. Credit or debit balances in a customer's account(s) may be offset by any other outstanding balance owed by or to the customer. Please allow 4 to 6 weeks for delivery. Offer available while quantities last.

Your Privacy: Steeple Hill Books is committed to protecting your privacy. Our Privacy Policy is available online at www.SteepleHill.com or upon request from the Reader Service. From time to time we make our lists of customers available to reputable third parties who may have a product or service of interest to you. If you would prefer we not share your name and address, please check here. ☐

BIABLPS09PI

LARGER-PRINT BOOKS!

GET 2 FREE LARGER-PRINT NOVELS PLUS 2 FREE MYSTERY GIFTS

Love Inspired.
SUSPENSE
RIVETING INSPIRATIONAL ROMANCE

Larger-print novels are now available...